Cornerstone of Love

CORNERSTONE
OF *Love*

Susan Carlisle

Dedication

To Kelsey, the perfect niece-in-law.

Dear Reader,

I can't begin to tell you how tickled I am to be sharing with you my *Modern Masters of Their Castles* series. I been developing *Cornerstone of Love, Designs on Forever* and a *His Heart's Home* for longer than I wish to admit. I love the strong alpha males with their I'm-in-control attitudes that soften because of the smart, savvy and sassy woman of Historical Restoration and Designs who tame them.

I did much of my research for these books during a visit to England where the goal was to visit a castle a day and have tea at a special place each afternoon. It was a wonderful trip. We even spent the night in a castle. I was in heaven. I combined the appearances of the castles we visited to develop the settings for each of the books. This first one centers on the oldest type of castle, or fortress called a keep. It needs some repair but the lord of the manor isn't sure the American woman sent to take care of that matter has what it takes to do so. He soon learns she can more than handle herself.

I am so happy with these stories from my heart and I hope you enjoy them as well.

Please share your thoughts on social media and if you have time give the book a review on Amazon, Barnes and Noble and/or Goodreads.

As always I love to hear from my readers.

Susan

CHAPTER ONE

"Bloody hell!" A deep British male voice barked from behind Allison Moore. "Have you lost your mind? Get down from there."

She gasped as powerful hands encircled her waist. "How dare you. Who do you think you are?"

"Don't you have better sense than to stand on this wall? It's already crumbling. You could fall." The fierce words were whispered close to her ear.

Allison forced herself not to struggle as her work boots dangled a moment before coming to rest on the slate roof of the castle. "Didn't your mother teach you never to manhandle a woman?"

"I'm not manhandling, just making sure you're safe." He rasped.

"I've no intention of falling. Let me go." Allison worked to keep her words even as she made another useless effort to get a good look at the man. Just as quickly as she had been seized, he released her. The air at her back cooled. Allison swiftly turned.

Tall and lean, he stood a head above her. A gust

of wind whipped at the toffee-colored locks on his forehead despite his effort to push them into place. He wore a business suit that could have only been tailor-made from the way it fit across his broad shoulders. Everything about him exuded authority. And sex appeal.

Allison retreated a step.

Offering an upturned hand, he said, "Don't move. You're not far from the edge."

She glanced over her shoulder, past the hip-high stone wall to the circular gravel drive sixty feet below. A gray roadster sat parked next to her blue rental car. She shifted to a safer position.

His forceful expression eased, making him even more handsome. His full mouth quirked upward on one side. "Are you the new contractor? My estate manager said I would find you up here. I'm Ian Chalmers, Earl of Hartley."

So, this was the owner of Hartley Castle. The newspapers pictures didn't do him justice. He appeared more impressive in person. Allison straightened her shoulders and extended her hand. "I'm Allison Moore, with Historic Restorations and Designs. My company has been retained to restore your tower."

He took her fingers in a firm grasp. "Surely, you know it's unsafe to walk on the walls."

When he released her hand, she had a fleeting sensation of disappointment. "I'm experienced at doing so. It's part of my job."

"That may be true," he gave her a pointed glare, "but accidents do happen. I'd rather one not occur from the top of my castle. What exactly do you do at uh..."

"Historic Restorations and Designs. I'm the

structural engineer in charge of this project. I'll be overseeing the reconstruction."

"Is that so?" His forehead wrinkled as he studied her. "You aren't at all what I had expected."

Allison stopped herself from rolling her eyes. That wasn't the first time she'd heard something like that.

He continued to watch her. "You don't fit the stereotypical contractor."

"Is that so?" Allison mimicked his words knowing full well he referred to her gender. Men generally made up the world of historical reconstruction. She and her partners continued to work hard to change that perception.

His lips twisted slightly, not quite becoming a smile. "For one thing, you're a woman. And since you are from America where there are no ancient keeps, I'm not sure how knowable you can be about mine."

Allison nodded, then swallowed the words begging to bubble out. She met his chauvinistic remark with a bold one of her own. "Lord Hartley, I can assure you that I'm more than capable of handling this job. Despite my nationality and sex."

He held up his hand. "I didn't mean to insult you. I merely made an observation. As the head of the Hartley family, I'm responsible for seeing our heritage is maintained and restored in the most skilled and factually accurate manner possible. I take my duty very seriously."

Allison lowered her chin. His questioning of her skills grated on her nerves, but she would let that go for now. And prove him wrong. "I understand your concerns." She waited until his beautiful ice-blue eyes met hers again. "Lord

Hartley, I assure you I'm capable of overseeing this project."

He lifted a brow. "You have experience repairing fourteenth century keeps?"

"I do. Years' worth." The temptation to stomp her foot in frustration filled her. Instead, she stayed cool and professional. "Before I started my company, I worked with a number of well-respected historical architectural firms all over the world. I've been a partner and founder in my own business for the past six years. And by the way, you don't need to live in or own a castle to appreciate how they're built."

The lord's expression turned thoughtful. "That was quite an impassioned speech, but I'm still not convinced your company's right for this job."

"Is that based on our resume or my appearance? I understood that my company had already been approved. We have a contract. I have supplies ordered and stone masons lined up. Otherwise, I wouldn't be here." A drop of moisture hit her cheek and she wiped it away. Another late spring rain. Something else she'd have to contend with if she managed to keep this project.

The lord's intent gaze shifted to the sky. "Let's get out of the wet. We can finish this discussion in my office."

Allison glanced around the castle roof, then refocused on him. "By the way," she tilted her head to the side, "do you regularly rescue people from the top of your castle?"

"No, but I don't usually have women climbing on *my* castle wall. In that, you are unique." A charming grin curved his lips.

Her stomach flipped. She rather liked that

compliment.

The man could charm when he put his mind to it.

Lord Hartley ducked through the arched opening and descended the winding stone stairway. Allison followed, mindful of the damp, steep, and narrow steps. Even with rubber-soled shoes, she treaded carefully. If she fell, no doubt Lord Hartley would show her to the door. She lagged a little behind. When she came out of the passage, he waited in the hall. His lips had formed a thin line. She suspected he didn't make a habit of waiting on anyone.

"Ms. Moore, this way." He turned, taking long strides down the carpeted hall.

Did he really just speak to her as if he were the schoolmaster, and she the disobedient child? Still, she couldn't help but find Lord Hartley's soft burr of an accent pulling at her, making her think of warm nights by a fire.

Allison stood still for a moment and collected herself before she entered into a discussion with Lord Hartley again. Temped to shout, "Who died and made you king?" she reminded herself the HRD couldn't afford to antagonize a client. Especially one with his clout. She'd settle for mouthing the words behind him. He might run his world, but he didn't run hers.

"Yes." Allison hurried to catch up.

She watched as his strong, loose-hipped strides took him along the stone corridor past enormous portraits that hung on either side of the walls. His ancestors, no doubt. As he walked, the slit in his finely tailored suit coat flipped open, giving her a glimpse of his behind. A nice one. But a good backside didn't negate his distrust of her abilities.

With an effort, she matched her pace to his. He took quick, sure steps down the main stone staircase into the great hall, then disappeared through a doorway.

Allison entered a small room lined with books to find Lord Hartley behind an enormous desk holding his mobile phone. The space suited him. Had it been established as a show of importance— or provide intimidation? Everything about Lord Hartley implied everyone obeyed him.

With a nod of his head, he motioned her toward one of the two burgundy leather chairs facing the desk. Settling comfortably, she crossed one leg over the other, just as confident in her abilities as he was in his position.

Did she want to work for him? He'd already irritated her with his assumptions of her skills. Would he always expect her to prove herself? Question her decisions? While growing up, her father had done that; pushed her into his ideas instead of letting her decide. She'd promised herself she wouldn't live under anyone else's expectations. Her job, her life, she was completely capable of running it all.

If she couldn't work with Lord Hartley, could HRD take the financial hit if they lost him as a client? Or the poor publicity Lord Hartley might give them? Allison, Mallory, and Jordon had worked too hard for Allison to destroy their reputation because of her inability to get along with one self-important earl.

Allison took a cleansing breath, letting it out slowly. On second thought, she'd have to figure out some way to make this work. It was too vital to her life plan and the future of the company.

Still, some jobs, some clients, weren't worth the trouble. Lord Hartley and his castle might fall into that category. She'd had difficult clients. Her focus on historical projects threw her into the world of the rich and entitled often. Yet something about Lord Hartley made him seem a little more exacting than others. Would he second guess every move she made?

The repair presented a challenge, and she did enjoy one of those. Could she convince him she was the man—*person*—for the job?

"Roger, I'm not convinced that the firm you hired is the correct one," he spoke into the phone. "I told you to hire a top-rated firm to repair the west tower. This project has to be done right and with no issues." There was another pause. "Yes, yes, she's sitting right here. Yes, I'll discuss it with her." Lord Hartley hung up.

The *tick, tick, tick* of the large walnut clock standing against the opposite wall echoed in the cavern-sized silence.

He took a seat in the desk chair, then formed a temple with his fingers at his mouth. His actions drew her attention to his full, wide lips. She bet they could form a beautiful smile, but rarely did. *What are you doing, Allison?*

"So, Ms. Moore, tell me about your company." Lord Hartley intended to interview her? Did he micromanage all areas of his world?

She would go along with it. Easy when she believed in her company. "Historic Restorations and Designs has been in business for six years. I've two partners. We each specialize in different areas of restoration. I handle the construction side. My partner Mallory Andrews oversees the historical design and Jordon Glass, our architect. In three years, we've become one of the foremost authorities in the field of heritage repairs. In the package sent to your estate manager, you'll find recommendations from previous happy clients, along with contact information. Feel free to reach out about their experience with us. We're currently based out of North Carolina, but rarely there."

His brow rose. "Currently?"

"Yes. We've plans to move the office to another state in the next six months, but that won't change any services we provide." In fact, they were doing so well, they anticipated expanding the company. But none of that related to the work she'd do for him. "You'll receive the best job possible."

Lord Hartley pursed his lips and nodded as if digesting that information. "Now tell me about some of the projects that you have personally supervised."

"I've overseen an entire villa restoration along with my partners in Italy. I've also managed a manor house renovation in Sussex, one in Scotland, and another in Wales. Oh, yeah, two more in France." She finished with, "Of course, this information, along with before and after pictures are included in the packet as well."

"I'm sure they are, but I want to hear it from you. Tell me about your most difficult project?" He continued to watch her as if trying to figure her out.

Allison didn't think she was that complicated. She had a job to do, and she had the skills to carry it out. "One of the manor houses in France. For a number of reasons."

"They were?"

She shrugged. "The language difference and a difficult owner. I got it done. When finished the manor house had been transformed into a beautiful hotel. I hear it's fully booked year-round." She didn't try to keep the pride out of her voice.

He nodded. "What about you?"

"Me?"

"Yes, tell me about you."

"I'm a graduate of MIT, top of my class. Growing up, I lived in a dozen countries around the world and developed a fascination with ancient structures. I've studied them in and out. That's why I'm the expert at our company in this type of reconstruction and why I'm the best engineer to complete your project."

"I like an employee with confidence. I'm going to give my decision further thought."

"I appreciate your thoroughness, but please recognize I can't wait around for too long. I arrived ready to start this project right away, and now you're implying you aren't sure. Please understand if you decide to break our contract there will be a penalty involved along with my expenses to date."

She stood and pulled her business card from her trouser pocket. "My cell number. Call me when you have made a decision. I can find my way out."

Ian's brow furrowed as he watched Allison Moore stride out of his office. She interested him. Her strength of will and determination intrigued him. She acted as if she knew her mind. Maybe she did have the fortitude and talent to get the repair done.

For all these strengths, her petite size captivated him. His hands had completely circled her waist when he had lifted her. Her tininess contradicted the type of work she supervised. Her red hair held by a band on the top of her head, gave her a fresh young appearance that belied her responsibility. Her heart-shaped face held vivid emerald eyes that could snap. He'd experienced that first hand.

Not at all what he'd expected in a construction engineer.

The charcoal gray pin-striped suit she wore with a white scooped-neck shirt hadn't detracted from her femininity. If anything, it enhanced her figure. The work boots broke the business effect. She must have changed into them to climb around on the tower. That, at least, showed common sense on her part.

Women in the trades didn't normally earn this much thought from him. Maybe it was her expressive eyes? Or the way she had stood up to him? Few outside his family dared that privilege.

She'd accused him of being chauvinistic. He'd not intended to come off that way. She'd surprised him. Normally he kept his thoughts to himself, but this time he'd blurted them out.

Spending his time thinking about Ms. Moore was counterproductive. Concentrating on the west tower repair should be his focus. He would discuss Ms. Moore with Roger tomorrow and settle the matter.

Roger had taken over the position of the Midland's estate manager after his father had died, ten years ago. A bachelor, Roger lived in a cottage on the estate and could keep an eye on the reconstruction. Roger loved the castle as well. He was as much family as employee.

Ian lips formed a rueful smile. Was Allison

Moore really the right man for the job? He huffed. The right person, he corrected himself. She definitely wasn't a man.

Shrugging out of his jacket, he tossed it over a chair, loosened his tie, and unbuttoned the top button of his shirt. His cell phone rang, and he answered.

"Hello, Clarissa."

"Hello, big brother. How're you doing?"

"I'm fine. It's nice to hear from you. How are the kids?"

"They're well. Soon out of school for the summer. I wondered if we could spend the break at the castle."

It didn't surprise him she wanted to come for the break. Up until his father and brother had died, they had spent most of their holidays and summers at the estate. Their family's getaway. Even with the sense of history and heritage, an escape to the country, wandering fields and horses and sheep and more. As kids, they'd delighted in their trips to the castle. "I don't see why not. Be aware, though, that I'm having the western tower fixed."

"The one that's falling down? Why now?"

"Six hundred years takes its toll. It's past time I put it to rights. Father always said the castle's our heritage, and that makes it my job to keep it in good repair."

"And the ever-loyal lord's taking care of it. Dotting each i and crossing every t. You know, Ian, that when the lordship fell to you, it didn't mean you had to become as old and stuffy as the title."

Someone had to take Hartley Shipping in hand after their father and older brother's tragic accident. Otherwise, he, his mother, and his sister wouldn't have had a roof over their heads or the family home. "I could always find you a place where you might help out. Make the business less stuffy."

"Thanks, but no thanks. The kids are enough for me to handle. John certainly isn't going to do his part."

Ian rolled his shoulders. He stopped himself from saying what he really wanted to concerning Clarissa's ex-husband. Ian hadn't thought much of John before Clarissa married him, and John had proved him right. Ian had done what he could to stop the marriage, wanting his sister to think things through. Then Clarissa eloped, and that was that. "Have you spoken to Mother lately? She isn't returning my calls."

"I talked to her a few days ago. She's off with some man she met while on the Riviera. When she calls, I'll tell her to phone you."

Great. More money wasted in his mother's search for happiness. He had failed his father and the family name the most where his mother was concerned. Ian walked to the window and stood with his feet apart, a hand crammed into his pocket. He gazed out over the lush lawn covered in a misty rain without really seeing it. "Thanks. I worry about her."

"You worry about us all." Clarissa paused. "We give you a hard time, but we do love you."

Ian's heart lightened. "And I love you too. It'll be good to see you and the kids. Maybe the west tower will be completed by then."

"Great. I'll be in touch before we come. Bye."

Ian dropped his phone into his pocket. Now he had another reason to finish the tower. A nice surprise for Clarissa and the children for them to have a new suite of rooms to stay in. If he wanted that to happen, someone needed to start the job right away. Ms. Moore?

Right now, he needed a pint and time away from his concerns. Leaving the office, he climbed the stairs two at a time to his bedroom to change clothes. Returning downstairs, he found Mrs. White, the castle housekeeper and cook. "I'm going out. Please hold my dinner."

Allison glanced around the dark pub of the Horse and Hound Inn in Hartshire after placing her order at the bar. She chose a table in the corner where she wouldn't be disturbed. From her vantage point, she watched people as they came in for a meal, and the men—all men for some reason—who trickled in to have a drink.

A few minutes earlier, she'd left the castle out of sorts confused by Lord Hartley's attitude. From the estate manager, she'd understood she had the job. Now the lord acted as if she didn't. This runaround was unacceptable. If he didn't come to a decision tomorrow, she would cut her losses and leave. She hated to do that. Quitting wasn't in her DNA. When she made up her mind to do something, she saw it through.

She studied the construction of the pub as she waited on her food. The inn had been built in the Tudor style of half-timbers, with low ceilings and dark support beams. She loved that type of work. Her room upstairs, despite being small, was adequate and homey. Inns like this one made the constant travel more bearable, even pleasant, since she visited England often on assignments. Having a pub attached to the inn also offered a convenient place for a meal. The atmosphere only added to the charm of the place.

A girl served Allison's beef pie as the door from the outside opened. A man ducked his head. *Lord Hartley.*

Allison's blood ran faster. She hadn't expected him.

Two men at the bar called "Ian, cheers," holding their tankards up in greeting. The bartender placed a mug on the counter for Ian.

She liked his name. It suited him. Country earl and all.

"Hello, mates," he responded in his deep, refined voice.

The lord looked different dressed in a cable sweater, tan twill pants, and jacket with a leather collar and patches on the elbows. Somehow more approachable. His hair had fallen over his brow and he pushed fingers through the unruly mane, mussing it more.

Giving the men at the bar a broad smile, Ian joined them. He carried himself with a lord-of-the-manor attitude. It wasn't so much that he acted above the others but that he stood out regardless, drawing attention. He certainly had hers.

Shaking off that idea, Allison made a point of focusing on her meal. Enough sparring between the two of them today.

"The next round's on me, lads," Lord Hartley said.

Allison quivered. The deep, rich accent grabbed her, drew her to the man with a beautiful voice. Give them an English accent, and she was a goner. Already Lord Hartley's warm timber had been embedded in her memory. She wouldn't be surprised if she heard it in her dreams.

After reading the local tabloids, she'd learned she wasn't the only one who liked his voice. The magazines often featured Ian Hartley with a tall, willowy model or a date from the British aristocracy and always attending the latest social event of the season.

Just as often, an article in the business pages described how he'd orchestrated another business merger. A young earl at thirty-six, he carried all the history and peerage that went with the title, along with heading a very successful international shipping business. Allison couldn't help but be impressed. Even if she wasn't sure about working for him. Their first meeting had confirmed his autocratic style and the articles established his demanding work ethics.

During her meal, Allison's gaze kept drifting to the bar. Ian and the others enjoyed themselves, telling stories, and laughing.

"You remember when we were boys, and Ian bet us that he could walk across the river and never get his clothes wet?"

A roar of laughter filled the room.

Her interest pricked; Allison listened closely.

Another man took up the tale. "Aye, and he did it, too. Until we realized that a log rested below the surface. We pushed him in. He was all wet for sure then." Boisterous whoops bounced off the ceiling beams.

Lord Hartley joined in. "I had you, I did. Until Mr. Forman walked across right behind me."

From where she sat, she noticed his sly smile. He had charisma; she'd give him that. And a nice laugh. Deep and raspy and whiskey smooth. She grinned to think of the stuffed-shirt of a man she'd dealt with that afternoon once a mischievous boy. What had happened in his life to make him so serious? Or had he covered his humor well when dealing with her? She took her final bite when he turned. Their gazes locked.

Ian placed his drink on the counter. With cheetah-like grace, he raised himself off the stool and started toward her. One corner of his mouth turned up. He had a hand stuffed into one pants pocket looking all virile male. Allison deliberately stared at her fork as she placed it on her plate. Bring her hand to her throat, she began running the charm on her necklace back and forth.

Another man almost as good-looking as the earl, who had been driven to make his place in the world, had hurt her. She wouldn't let that happen again. The next man she agreed to have a relationship with would need to care about her more than how he appeared to others.

"Why, Ms. Moore, are you enjoying our local food? Nancy's is one of the finest cooks around."

Allison tipped her head to meet his eyes. "Yes."

Two of the men from the bar sauntered up behind him.

"I hope we haven't disturbed your meal." The earl's intense gaze didn't leave her.

"Lord Hartley," she said with emphasis. She stood; the wooden chair made a scraping noise. "No, you didn't. An excellent meal. Now, if you'll excuse me." She stepped around him.

A roar of laughter sprouted from his friends as they slapped him on the shoulder. One crowed, "So, Ian, are you losing your touch with the birds?"

They whooped with merriment again.

Allison stopped and focused on Ian's friends. "I'm *not* one of his women. I'm an engineer here to oversee the repair of the castle tower."

"Are you now?" the older of the two men said, glancing at Ian.

Ian shrugged. "She is."

"It's been a long day. So, I'll say goodnight." Crossing the pub, Allison climbed the stairs, pausing to peek over her shoulder. Lord Hartley watched her. A sizzling shiver slid along her spine.

CHAPTER TWO

An hour later, Allison shifted in her bedroom chair and crossed her arms over her chest as she looked at her laptop. The faces of Mallory and Jordon were on split screens. She continued speaking. "I wish I could tell him forget it, that we don't need his job. He's so...so..."

"Handsome?" Mallory watched her intently.

"Yes, but worse than that, he's arrogant. Not convinced I can do the job."

"Is that exactly what he said?" Jordon leaned in, her face growing larger. "I thought he was surprised you were a woman."

Allison begrudgingly agreed with Jordon. She tended toward the pragmatic. Jordon would never send Allison into an uncomfortable situation where a man was concerned.

"You've worked for self-important people before, so why does this one get your feathers so ruffled?" Mallory watched her as if trying to read her. Allison's friend had never met a man she couldn't handle. She wielded her beauty like a baseball bat and baffled them with her brains.

Maybe Allison needed to take a lesson from her about the brains part. "I don't know. For some reason, he rubs me the wrong way."

Mallory pursed her lips and nodded. "Interesting."

"What's interesting?"

"You understand that not every good-looking, intelligent man who challenges you will turn out like your dad. Or worse, like that jerk you dated."

"I'm not talking about dating Lord Hartley! I'm talking about working for him. Getting along with him."

"Al, we need this project." Jordon's tone remained even. "It's high profile, extending our reach, the money's really good, and your chance to take over as COO. We can hire someone to take your place with the fee we clear on the project."

Alison sighed. "About our plans, are you both sure you're good with them?"

"Are you kidding?" Mallory asked. "You'd take over all the tedious work that we've had to divide between us. I'll love focusing on my design work. I'm worried you might not like it. I believe you'll miss your side of things."

"I might, but sleeping in my own bed every night will make up for it. Plus, I can take on small projects close to home to keep me busy."

"I want that for you too, Al," Jordon joined in. "We've got a solid plan in place. Just don't mess it up by making Lord Hartley mad."

"Got it. I know this project's important. I'm

afraid he's going to try to micromanage it. Me."

"Yeah, and we know how you like to run the show," Jordon said softly. She and Mallory had accused her of that often. She guessed she'd learned that from her drill sergeant father.

Mallory grinned. "I've complete confidence in your ability to win him over. Show him you have the stuff to do the job."

"I do have that. Okay, I'll try again in the morning. Give him my best pitch to why our firm and I, in particular, can take care of his needs."

Mallory raised a brow. "That's an interesting turn of phrase."

Allison huffed. "You know what I mean. This isn't about an attraction, but a job. I'll do my best to get along with the master of the castle. The money and his endorsement would mean a lot to us. I won't let you down. I hope. I've got to get some sleep, but before I go, how're your projects progressing?"

"I hope mine's finished in a month. I do love Belgium. I may stay afterward to explore," Mallory said.

That was so like her, forever searching for the next great find. "Sounds like a good plan. What about you, Jordon?"

"I'm headed to west of York to give an investment banker an estimate on redoing his manor house. A long-term job if we get it."

"We need to make plans to get together soon. Have an 'in person' board meeting," Allison suggested. "Maybe near a beach."

"I'm in," Mallory said.

"Me too." Jordon nodded.

"I love you guys."

"Back at you. Bye." Mallory waved and her face disappeared.

"I love you too. Talk soon." Jordon clicked off.

Allison looked at the blank screen. Mallory and Jordon expected her to come through for them and the company. She needed to make that happen. Lord Hartley would have to get on board with her plan.

Allison fought through the cobwebs of jetlag sleep from her trip over from America the day before. Someone knocked on her door. Opening one eye, she glanced at the clock on the bedside table. Six a.m. Who in the world?

"One minute," she mumbled, resisting the urge to pull the duvet over her head.

She flipped on the small bedside lamp and drew the matching hot pink robe over the pajama set her parents had given her for Christmas. "Who is it?"

"Ian Hartley."

Her nerves went to attention. What did he want at this hour? She ran her hands through her hair to tame it. Cinching her robe, she cracked the door. "Yes?"

"I'm sorry, but I need to talk to you. I tried to call, but no answer."

"I didn't hear my phone." Who did he think he was? What kind of person came to someone's door at this hour? "It's early."

"Could I stand somewhere besides the hallway to have this discussion?"

Allison's lips drew into a line. "I'll meet you in

the pub. Give me time to dress."

"I have to catch a flight," he checked his sleek gold watch, "in less than an hour. This won't take long. I don't have the time to wait, and I know how long it can take for a woman to dress."

"Oh, really? You don't know anything about me, Lord Hartley." She made a move to close the door.

Using a hand, he stopped her and gave her a pleading look. "I'm sorry if I have insulted you in some way. With a sister and mother, I've waited more than my fair share for them to think they are presentable. I just need a minute."

Seeing his sincerity, she relented with a huff. "Okay. Just for a minute. Come in."

Entering, he brought a hint of citrus with him and closed the door behind him. His piercing gaze met hers. "Some pressing business came up and I must leave. I want to have the tower repair arrangements settled before I go."

He remained near the door. She studied him a moment. This morning he looked dashing in a tailored navy business suit that accented his broad shoulders and chest. The power tie she would've expected was missing, and his collar stood open. He portrayed the appearance of casual British well-to-do superbly. Allison pulled her housecoat closer around her, feeling inadequate standing in her pajamas. Her attention returned to his face.

She watched as his gaze traveled from the top of her head to the tips of her green painted toenails. When his attention lingered, her toes curled. Did he find her lacking like her ex-boyfriend Dan had?

The room narrowed down like a dollhouse with his large body inside it. Allison couldn't take a deep breath. Was he taking up more than his share of the air? Why did she have such a reaction to him? "I spoke to my partners last night. I told them your concerns, and they wanted to reassure you that our firm could see this project completed to your satisfaction."

"And I spoke to my manager minutes ago and have reviewed the packet you sent. Your credentials will do. I don't wish to waste more time locating another contractor."

Not exactly a vote of confidence, but she would take what she could get. He didn't apologize for his implications the day before, but he was eating crow nonetheless, and she liked it.

"I'd like you to start on the job ASAP."

Yesterday he'd stalled with transparent concerns, and now he couldn't have her doing the work fast enough. His high-handed attitude rubbed her wrong. Did everyone drop everything to meet his demands? Judging by his overbearing nature, it would be *for* and not with. So much for taming the outrageous autocratic earl.

"I'll start right away. I'd like for you to understand that I have the final word where this project's concerned. I know the guidelines and the method of building."

He studied her for a moment. "Granted. But you need to understand that this is my ancestral home and it's my responsibility to care for it. I take that very seriously."

"I can appreciate that, Lord Hartley."

"While I'm gone if you need anything contact Roger." He checked his watch again, before his gaze shifted to her toes, now peeking out from under her pajama bottoms once more. His gaze roamed her body. His eyes had turned a deep ocean blue by the time they met hers.

His lips lifted into the sexiest smile she'd ever seen. Warmth built to a wave of heat before it crashed, to ripple throughout her body.

"Interesting polish color." He started toward the door then hesitated. "You know, I think all our meetings should be conducted early in the morning in your bedroom," he said. "I wouldn't need a cup of coffee to wake up."

A week later, Ian tightened his grip on the steering wheel as he rolled into the last turn of the narrow country road. Hartley Castle. There on the rise in the distance stood one of his many obligations in the late afternoon sun.

In his absence, erected scaffolding covered the south side. Giving the lawn an encompassing glance, he spotted stacks of materials as well. Allison Moore had certainly made progress. Roger's daily reports had been nothing but glowing about her efforts.

He continued up the long drive. A car parked in his usual spot by the main door. With a twist of the wheel, he sprayed gravel in an effort to miss the blue compact. With a jerk, he pulled alongside Ms. Moore's vehicle.

Stepping out of the car, he grabbed his briefcase and jacket then walked around to the side lawn toward the pallets of supplies. Voices above caught his attention. He couldn't quite make out what was being said, but the soft, southern American drawl he knew without a shadow of a doubt belonged to Ms. Moore.

Ian stepped far enough away from the castle

wall to see the top of the buttress. His gaze traveled along the gray stone and came to an abrupt stop. A flash of neon pink bobbed above the wall. Ian blinked. The spot of color moved closer to the edge. Ms. Moore wore a fuchsia hardhat.

She spoke to a heavyset bearded man standing beside her. "We need the stone here no later than Friday. The stonemasons will arrive Thursday evening."

Her voice carried clearly.

"I talked to the quarry this morning." The man's voice sounded agitated.

"Can they or can't they have a load of stone here on time?"

"No." He shrugged a shoulder. "A week at the earliest."

"I've worked with this company before. They should know what I expect. You call them first thing in the morning and tell them that won't be acceptable. Tell them you're speaking for me. If we must find another supplier, we will." She faced him directly, "Lord Hartley's expecting this project to move forward. So am I."

The man nodded curtly.

Less harshly, she continued. "Do you have any idea why all of a sudden there's a problem? You told me last week they said they could handle the order."

"I'm sorry, ma'am. I don't know the answer to that."

Raising her hand, she pointed above her head toward the damaged side of the tower. "I want the new scaffolding in place around the outside in the next two days."

The man nodded, his white hardhat shifting

back and forth. "Yes, ma'am. I'll get the men on it first thing in the morning. Evening, ma'am."

Ms. Moore certainly was the man uh... woman in charge. She hadn't exaggerated when she'd told him that she could run the project. For a second there, he felt sorry for her foreman.

He'd thought of her snapping green eyes and fiery hair one too many times in the last week. And those adorable toes that had peeked out from under her pajama pants.

She acted nothing like his ex-wife who had showed little interest in the Hartley holdings outside of the prestige and money it gained her. He couldn't remember a time that Judith had given a fig for anything but herself. She'd been all that was proper and suitable in a wife by British society standards. In every area except one – remaining faithful.

Ms. Moore thought outside the box. Green polish on her toes. Pink hat on her head. He wasn't used to dealing with such a strong-willed woman. Maybe that's why he and Ms. Moore hadn't warmed up to each other at their first meeting. One thing was for sure she wasn't an easy woman. And the direct opposite of the type of woman he should want. Yet he did want...

When the time came—when he had to marry again to continue the bloodline—it wouldn't be to someone like Ms. Moore. He wanted a woman pleasing to live with, who met the criteria. Someone like Ms. Moore would offer her opinion, diverting, and always challenging him. Highly unsuitable. So why did she have such a pull on him?

She removed her hat and set it on the edge of the battlement. Flipping her head from side to side, she slung her hair around. Ian couldn't take his eyes off her, as she finger-combed the wavy, flaming mass. The late sun made it almost glow. This view with her hair in disarray and the sky a darkening blue took his breath.

Moments went by before she stopped in mid-movement and looked down. Despite the distance, it was as if they stood face to face.

She had the look of a wild thing, as if she loved life and wanted to live it to the fullest. His life consisted of serious ideals like duty and honor to his family. Where he marched through life, she weaved through it. Something about Ms. Moore made him nervous, a little off-center.

Yet she drew him to her. Like jumping off a cliff for the thrill but understanding it might kill him. But the chance to experience her might be worth the pain. Would she let him find out?

Uncomfortable with his thoughts, Ian gave her a sharp salute. She jerked her hands out of her hair and dipped her chin in acknowledgment. Their gazes held for seconds longer before he pointed down and toward the front door. She dropped her chin in understanding.

"Well, I've been summoned by the lord of the castle," Allison mumbled, wrinkling her nose.

During his absence, he'd called daily to check on the progress of the repairs. And spoke only to Roger. Not once had she talked to the man herself. Did Lord Hartley hold his original opinion of her ability to run the job?

Happily, she'd reported daily to Roger. And so far, the reports stressed the positive. The first days she'd devoted to lining up her crew and ordering materials. HRD tried to use local workers whenever possible. It kept the overall costs down, as well as the benefit of getting local expertise.

The pastoral view around her gave her a moment of peace. Lord High and Mighty could wait a little longer. Sitting on the edge of the stone, she let her body relax. Minutes later, she stood, squared her shoulders, and took a deep breath. She needed to prepare for her meeting. Though confident Lord Hartley would try to intimidate her; she had no intention of allowing him to do so.

Making no effort to hurry, she descended the winding stairway, as she reviewed her report. It wouldn't hurt the man to have to cool his heels a little longer. The thought that he might pace the hall brought a grin to her lips.

As she descended the staircase, the soles of her heavy boots thumped. Lord Hartley stood holding a stack of mail while he looked up at her. Allison hesitated, and their gazes met briefly, before she continued down. Shifting her fuchsia hardhat from one hand to the other, she approached him. She loved the hat color. It always made a statement. Stiffening her spine, she tucked the hat securely in the crook of her arm, ready to deal with "the master of the castle."

Still as astonishingly striking as she remembered, he wore tailored slacks that hugged his hips. His shirt sleeves were rolled up, letting his muscular forearms show. Small lines and faint dark smudges lingered around his eyes. Studying him closer, he seemed tired. Somehow it made him more appealing. Human, even.

When he didn't immediately look at her, Allison cleared her throat. He flopped the mail onto the tall table beside him before giving her his full attention. She jerked. His gaze caught hers and held. Under such intense scrutiny, she questioned why she didn't prefer it when he paid her no attention. Warmth crept up her neck. If she wasn't careful, this man could devour her thoughts. Something she couldn't afford or wouldn't allow.

He continued to watch her. Was he judging her florescent green T-shirt with the HRD logo on the pocket or her well-worn cargo pants? Dan had questioned her femininity when he'd seen work clothes. Her hands-on approach often had her looking less than pristine, as well as leaving her hands rough to the touch. He'd complained about that as well. She resisted the urge to wipe her palms on her pants.

The lord's brows knitted together as he focused on her boots. His lips quirked upward. Was he thinking how distasteful? The intense perusal he gave her worked its way up her again until his gaze met hers. Disgusted or amused? Either way, she didn't appreciate being made fun of. "Problem?"

"Not with anything I've seen," he said in a rough, honey tone. A tingle shot through her. Somehow, he'd made that statement sound more personal than business-related. "Though I'm disappointed not to see those green-tipped toes once more."

He didn't seem to mind the way she looked. How should she feel about that?

Moving away, he said in a cool tone, "So, Ms. Moore, I see you've started the repair moving forward."

"I have."

"I'm interested in a detailed report. Will you please join me for dinner here tonight to discuss the progress to date and your immediate plans?"

Having put in a long day, dodging the occasional shower and fleeting sun, Allison looked forward to a bath, a solid meal, and curling up in bed with a good book. She didn't want to spar with this man. She should be fresh when taking him on. "I've had a difficult day. Do you mind if we meet in the morning?"

"I do mind. I've other things scheduled then."

"If you insist."

"I do."

Allison gritted her teeth in an effort not to lose her temper. Why couldn't he give a little? She turned toward the front door.

When she passed him, he briefly touched her arm. The spot heated. "I shall expect you here at eight." Not waiting for a reply, he picked up the mail again.

Allison crossed the great hall, making her way to the exit. Opening the heavy door, she stepped out. Yeah right, dinner with a man who disturbed her on more than one level. An evening not to look forward to. At all.

A few hours later, Ian watched from the lawn as Allison's car came roaring up the drive. The compact threw gravel as she pulled beside his vehicle. Ian stalked toward her. He barked as she slid from the seat, "Who taught you to drive?"

"What?" Her face and voice held pure innocence.

"Your driving is atrocious. Did you learn at a car track?" Ian came to stand beside her, hands on his hips.

She looked from him to the car and back, giving him a sweet smile. "No. In Italy."

"Right," he muttered deflated. That figured.

She offered him no more explanation. Shaking his head, he went to the castle door, opened it, and waited. "Come in. Mrs. White should have dinner ready."

Ms. Moore walked by him in a way that avoiding touching him. Was she afraid of him? Or was she as affected by him as he was her?

He glanced at her shoes. She'd replaced her chunky boots with white-leather tennis shoes. Ian couldn't help but be disappointed. He'd hoped to see her pretty toes. Some men liked breasts and other men liked legs, but he had a thing for feet.

She dipped her head. Was she hiding a grin? "After you Ms..." He stopped and looked directly at her. "May I call you Allison?"

"Okay." She didn't sound excited about the idea.

"You may call me Ian." He joined her in the foyer. "This way." He guided her to the dining room where the table had been set for three.

"Someone else is joining us?" She sounded relieved by the idea.

The thought that she might be concerned about being alone with him disturbed him. For some reason, he wanted Allison to like him. Ian went to a chair and pulled it out. "Roger will be here in a minute. He's taking a call."

Seconds later, Roger entered the room. "Hello, Allison."

"Hi, Roger. Working hard or was that a girl on the line?"

Roger chuckled. "Now, I don't kiss and tell."

"You two have obviously gotten to know each other well." Ian didn't like the easiness between them. Allison didn't act prickly around Roger. So maybe it was just him. His reaction resembled jealousy, too close for his comfort. Why did the thought of a relationship between his trusted friend and this woman he really didn't know disturb him? Maybe if she got to know him better things would relax between them. He scolded himself. Allison purpose here was to do a job, not become his friend. "Shall we eat?"

Ian took the seat at the head of the table. Allison sat to his left, leaving Roger the chair on the right. Mrs. White entered carrying a tray holding plates filled with roast beef and vegetables.

"I assume you've already met Mrs. White." Ian glanced from one woman to the other.

"Oh yes, the miss has spent—"

Allison interrupted her. "Yes, Mrs. White's very welcoming. I'll have to buy new clothes if I keep eating her cooking."

Mrs. White placed the tray on the hunt board. "It's a pleasure to cook for someone who stays around long enough to enjoy it." She gave Ian a pointed look then served Allison before moving around the table to him, then Roger. Afterward, she quietly left them to their meal.

As they started eating, Ian said, "I understand from Roger's daily reports the project's progressing well." For the first time that evening, Allison seemed enthusiastic. He liked that look on her. "Please tell me your view of the restoration and how you think it's going and what problems you foresee."

Allison efficiently gave him a report. Ian wished that all his employees did so well. She finished with, "Currently, we're making the progress I expected. It takes time to get up and running, but major work will start in earnest on Monday morning. All my stone layers should arrive by Thursday afternoon."

"And you know these people personally?"

"Many of them. They're skilled artisans. About six have worked on my jobs before. I have three new hires who are coming from all over the country since this project's so large. That's what I've been doing for the past week. The only problem not solved is the lack of space to house some of the stone masons and their crews."

"How many?"

"I need rooms for four men."

Mrs. White returned with three plates, each holding a slice of cake. She placed one in front of their places.

Ian caught the interest on Allison's face. Moments later, he noticed her eyes closed over a look of pure bliss as Allison ate a second bite.

Did she have a similar reaction during other occasions? Would her eyes take on the same dreamy look and turn the color of the fields in spring when she was aroused? He'd like to find out. Bloody hell, where had that idea come from? Had it been so long between women that he was having thoughts about a stranger?

Thankfully, a question from Roger drew Ian from his inappropriate thoughts. "What are your plans?"

"I'll figure out something before the time comes."

Ian glared at her in disbelief. "Are you always that laid-back about problems?"

Roger cleared his throat.

"I have a few more days. Something will come together." She returned to her cake.

He couldn't understand her nonchalant attitude. Doing business like that was beyond him. If a problem arose, he wanted it solved and settled. Hoping it would all work out didn't sit with in his personality.

"Coffee, dear?" Mrs. White offered.

Allison shook her head. "No, thank you."

Ian's forehead wrinkled as if perplexed. "You don't drink coffee. You refused the wine earlier. What do you drink besides water?"

"A bit personal, don't you think?" Allison smiled sweetly.

Roger made a choking noise.

"If you must know I like tea, especially sweetened iced tea." Allison's response came out smooth and rich as silk, too much so. It was as if she were trying to control her tongue.

Ian stifled a smile. For some reason, he liked having her test him. Few rarely did. Without removing his gaze from Allison, he said, "Mrs. White, would you please bring our guest a cup of tea."

"No, thank you. I'm fine, really," Allison told the grinning Mrs. White. "But I thank you for the wonderful cake. The best I've ever had. I'd love to have the recipe."

A bright smile came to the older woman's face. "Thank you. I'll show you how to make it."

"That would be wonderful. I'd like to make it

for my family sometime."

Mrs. White left the room.

Ian's gut clenched. He glanced at Roger, who grinned and raised a brow, giving him no help. He'd assumed she was single. "You have a husband and children?"

"No. I'm not married, nor do I have any children. Just my mother and father, brother and sister, and their kids."

Relief washed through him. "They must miss you."

"They're used to me travelling. We don't get to spend much time together, but I plan to change that soon. I think I miss them more than they miss me."

He wanted to know personal details, which confused him. "You mentioned you were going to make changes after this job. Are you moving home?"

"More or less. I'm moving to my parents' hometown, buying my grandparents' home. They're moving to a retirement community."

"And what does that have to do with your office?" Roger asked.

Glad Roger asked, Ian feared his interest showed too much.

"I'll run HRD out of my house. Become the COO of the company. We've done our business by word of mouth, internet, and cell phones up to now, sharing all the tasks depending on who's free."

"Really?" Ian couldn't keep his surprise out of his voice.

She looked at him. "I hope that doesn't put us in a poor light."

Ian shook his head, his interest pricked.

"Our clients are a select group. We've worked through references from other companies and satisfied customers. We've a website and a virtual office. After a client explains what they want, we discuss who's best suited, or if we all need to pitch in."

"Interesting." Ian couldn't imagine running a company on such a stress-free concept. Hartley Shipping was a large, gangly operation. He wished for such simplicity in his work life. "What do you do about all the stuff like paperwork, taxes, billing?"

"We divide it up three ways. Each of us handles a part. Though I'll take it all on after the move."

"Fascinating." Ian couldn't help but be impressed. Their company ran like her—wild and free. Though that wouldn't work with things like housing workmen without putting any effort into it. Maybe he had the answer to that problem. He turned to Roger. "Isn't that cottage off the lane still empty?"

"Yes. I was going to put an ad in the paper to let it tomorrow."

"Is there any reason that a couple of men couldn't stay there? Allison would take one of the rooms here. That would get all the housing settled."

"Stay here?" Allison's voice went higher and thinner.

"Yes."

"I can't stay here!" A mixture of disbelief and anger surrounded her words.

"Why ever not? I assure you there's plenty of room." Ian watched her.

"I just can't."

"I think that's the wisest course. It'd also allow

you swift access if there were problems." Ian saw it as a sound plan. By the horrified look on Allison's face the plan didn't impress her.

Allison pushed her chair out and glared at him. "You can't so high-handily decide something that's my responsibility, and you certainly shouldn't decide where I live."

"The intent wasn't to tell you what to do but help remove a problem." Why the over-reaction?

"I'll take a couple of rooms in the next village instead. Thanks anyway."

Ian didn't understand her resistance. "Staying here is a practical solution. You'll be comfortable and well-rested, so you can focus on the repair."

Allison stood. "I can assure you that I always have a clear head where my work is concerned. I'll be fine with the arrangements I have in mind."

Ian rose as well. "Now, Allison. Hear me out. I didn't mean to insult you. Only trying to help." Why couldn't she see that? "Spend some time here and if it doesn't work, then you may move to the neighboring village. I don't expect you'll enjoy the two-hour round-trip drive much. We don't have wide straight roads in this area."

She looked at Roger.

He shrugged. "I'd think twice before I refused the offer, Allison. Ian's correct about the drive. It'll make for extra-long days for you. You'd be more comfortable here."

The room fell silent. She sighed. "Well, if you both think that's what I should do."

Allison seemed resigned to the idea. Ian didn't want her to resent him. Had he really stepped over the line, or was she just super sensitive? To placate her, he said, "If you stay here, you can show Mrs. White how to make your iced tea and have it available all the time."

She glared at him as if she wanted to say something, but she held her tongue. Finally, she said, "Then if you'll excuse me, I'll go pack. Please tell Mrs. White thank you for the lovely meal." Allison didn't wait for a response before she headed toward the door.

"Allison?" Roger's voice held an appeasing note. She turned. "This afternoon, you commented you wanted to review the work after the men... How did you put it? Knocked-off for the day. Staying here will give you a chance to do that."

Allison's lips drew into a tighter line, and she nodded before walking toward the door again.

Ian followed her, having to move quickly. He'd no idea that she would react this negatively to his suggestion. She efficiently found her way to the front door, never acknowledging him. As she approached it, he moved ahead and opened the door. She made a soft hiss as he brushed by.

He searched her face. "My intent was to help you."

She pinned him with a look. "Yet somehow I feel manipulated about a decision that should be mine. I don't like you dictating to me about personal affairs."

"I dictated nothing. You have the choice to say no."

She glowered at him. "Really? You would've accepted me not doing it your way?"

Ian shifted. Probably not. People who worked for him didn't speak to him the way she did. Allison was calling him on the carpet. He nodded. "Duly noted."

"I'd appreciate it if you'd let me take care of the project you *hire*d me to do. All of it. It'll go smoother and faster if you let me handle things from here on out."

Allison hurried down the steps. She had strapped herself in the car and had the door closed before he caught up with her. He tapped on the glass. She jolted then rolled down the window. Ian leaned over to see her clearly.

Wearing his best conciliatory smile, he met her gaze. "Allison, I believe if you allow yourself, you'll find staying at the castle pleasant and convenient."

She didn't say anything. Instead, she started the car, put it in gear, and sped out the drive.

An unnerving question lingering. Would he find it as pleasant and convenient?

CHAPTER THREE

The next morning Allison carried her battered luggage as she followed Mrs. White up the massive staircase of Hartley Castle to the second floor.

Allison had fallen in love with the ancient stone fortress. Even the damp aged smell delighted her. Strength lingered here. A lineage. Stability. Permanence. Like a medieval knight, it stood waiting to protect anyone who called it home. That kind of security was what she wanted in her life. A place always waiting for her return.

As Ian had led her to the dining room the night before the light filtering through the leaded glass windows high on the walls created a mesmerizing effect. The lit sconces along the way had helped bring out the red and gold color of the thick carpets covering the floor. He had held an immense oak door for her to enter the room. She had absorbed it all.

The dining room was a large space, but the

heavy dark timbers somehow made it less intimidating and more inviting. The table could easily seat twenty people. She had been sure that her comfortable-cotton-floral dress and sweater wouldn't be appropriate for the occasion, but it had been.

That was all she owned anyway in the dress-for-an-occasion wear. Functional and packable would be how she would describe her wardrobe. One more thing she planned to change when she had a home of her own.

At the top of the stairs, Mrs. White captured her attention again. She indicated to the right with her hand. "Your bedroom is this way."

Was Ian's bedroom in the same direction? Hopefully not. Surely it was down the hallway in the opposite direction. She didn't want to run into him. Just the sound of her name coming from his lips did peculiar things to her body, even when she was angry at him. The lilt he gave the last symbol touched her like a feathered caress. A tingle fluttered across her nerve endings, leaving a delicious warmth in its wake. Every time. Just a light touch of his fingers would fracture her mind so that she had to work to put the pieces back into smooth running order.

No, living in Hartley Castle wasn't going to make life easier for her. She did need plenty of rest to get this job done correctly, but she didn't see how sleeping in his home would be conducive to peaceful nights, especially if he were near. Yet she couldn't say that.

Mrs. White continued to chatter on about the history of the castle as they walked. Allison heard the love in the woman's voice for the keep and Ian's family.

"Mrs. White, how long have you worked at the castle?" Allison asked.

"Oh, since before Ian was born. Here we are. The green room," she said with almost a reverent tone as she pushed open the wooden door. "The master gave me instructions to give you this room. He thought you might like it best."

Ian had even made that decision as well? Just another area of her life he managed. The man must have an opinion on everything within his sphere of influence. She didn't like being told what to do in general, and Ian's highhanded invasion of her personal life appealed even less. She'd try to put up with Ian's intrusions for the company and her partners' sakes.

Her plan consisted of getting along and to stay out of his way. That shouldn't prove too difficult. Surely, he'd leave again soon. She couldn't imagine the head of a major company and the glossy page's most eligible bachelor of the English empire hanging around this far from the bright lights. Country living must be so dull for him.

She entered the green bedroom. Dark stone walls could give the illusion coldest, but in here with the lit lamps, the room took on a deep inviting glow. An enormous carved oak four-poster bed faced the door. Sea-foam-green drapes and a matching comforter gave the room its name. Flanked on each side of the bed, two deep-set windows viewed the meadows. A fireplace anchored another wall. She'd arrived in heaven.

"It's lovely," Allison said in a breathy voice. Even worth dealing with her roller-coaster emotions concerning Ian 24/7.

"The master's mother redid rooms in this wing.

This was Ian's boyhood room. The bath, which was updated last year with a Jacuzzi, is through there." Mrs. White pointed to a smaller door to the right. "The master isn't often here these days, but when he is, he usually has someone visiting with him. He wants his guests comfortable."

So, this room's where all of Ian's women, uh visitors stayed. The beautiful room lost some of its appeal. She shivered from the chill that settled over her. "Lord Hartley's visitors stay here? In this room?"

Mrs. White gave her a quizzical look. "Why no, dear. All visitors have stayed in the blue room. Across the hall. But you're more than an average visitor."

Why did that bit of information make Allison's heart jump? Her body warmed again. She could get used to this kind of living.

Excusing herself, Mrs. White left to attend to her duties. Allison unpacked her clothes, hanging her two simple dresses in the free-standing wardrobe. For some women, the wardrobe wouldn't have been enough closet space, but Allison saw it as part of the charm of living in a castle.

She gazed around the room, trying to imagine Ian as a young boy. Was he demanding and serious even then? Had he ever sat on the floor before the fireplace and pushed his little cars around? From what she'd heard at the pub quite possibly. Why had that side of Ian disappeared?

Dwelling on Ian wasn't what she needed to do. She had a job that demanded her attention. Keeping the repair on track would turn her goals into reality.

The next day at lunchtime, Ian pushed through

the swinging door into the kitchen and came to a stop. Before him, Allison stood behind the large wooden worktable. She had a smudge of flour on one cheek as if she'd brushed a lock of hair away. Her hands pushed and folded a mound of dough. Flour dust created small clouds in the air around her.

Her head didn't move, but she lifted her eyes. Their gazes met, held. She watched, waited. The corner of her mouth lifted slightly, almost in a question.

His gut tightened. Beautiful in a natural, fresh way, Allison had no idea of her power over him. He stood mesmerized by her perfection. She seemed as if she belonged there. An idea he'd no business having.

Less than forty-eight hours ago Allison arrived and her presence filled the castle. He'd left his bed wondering if he would see her at breakfast or in the hallway. He'd continually had to remind himself to concentrate on his work. Not his best idea to bring her here considering the attraction he felt toward her.

"I had no idea that restoration work included preparing dough." His tone held a note of censure. He felt more than saw Mrs. White's interest in them. Those initial moments of warmth disappeared like dew on a sunny day. Good. He didn't need cloudy judgment.

Allison punched the dough. "Is that your diplomatic way of questioning why I'm in the kitchen in the middle of the day instead of up on the tower?"

"I have to say I'm used to my employees staying on their assigned job."

Allison's shoulders straightened. "Why does that not surprise me? For your information, even the boss is allowed some time off. I've worked eighteen-hour days for the past week, so when Mrs. White offered to show me a couple of her recipes, I took her up on her offer. I can assure you that your money isn't being squandered."

Before he could comment, a phone rang. Allison blinked and looked away as Mrs. White hustled to answer it. Ian continued into the room, stopping across the counter from Allison.

"Yes, yes." Mrs. White hung up the phone.

Allison continued the kneading motion as if it were a natural extension of her arms. "Is something wrong?"

"My daughter is at the hospital. My granddaughter has had a bad bike accident. I must go."

Ian moved around the counter. "Can I do something? Drive you?"

"No, no. I'll be fine. I'll get your meal then go." Mrs. White went one way, and then the other.

Ian placed his hands on her shoulders. "You will not. I can take care of myself. You go."

"I'll get his lunch and clean up the kitchen." Allison pulled a large bowl to her and placed the dough in it. She covered it with a cloth. "I can also see to the evening meal."

"I'll help," Ian offered. "I don't have anything on until later this afternoon."

Mrs. White visibly relaxed. "Thank you. The roast and vegetables are already in the oven. All that's needed is the salad and the rolls. Soup's on the stove warming for lunch."

Allison wiped her hands on the apron she wore. "I'll take care of it all. Now, you go see about your family."

Without another word, Mrs. White bustled out the door.

Allison didn't glance his way. Instead, she went to the refrigerator. "I must knead this other dough, then I can serve your lunch."

"I assure you I can see to my own lunch." Ian stepped to the cabinets in search of a bowl. "I'm not helpless."

"If you say so." Allison placed the extra-large glass bowl on the counter and started spreading flour over the surface.

Ian leaned a hip against the counter, watching her.

After she rolled the blob of dough out of the bowl onto the dusted area, she began to push and pull the mass, adding a handful of flour now and then.

"That looks therapeutic."

"I'll have to admit I've taken out my aggression on dough more than once."

Ian winced. "Like a few minutes ago?"

She gave him a direct look and a small smile. "Maybe so."

Allison went to work. He continued to watch her fingers manipulate the dough. What would it feel like to have those same hands doing that across his shoulders? He had to control those types of thoughts. Had to.

She glanced at him. "You want to try? See if you can get rid of some of your frustration?"

He blinked. Could she see that? He'd thought

he'd covered it well. "I don't think so."

"Aw, come on. Live a little. Take a chance. It helps."

"I can take a dare. What do I need to do?"

Allison grinned, and he had the funniest feeling he'd been had. "Wash your hands. Then take some flour and dust it over them."

Ian did so then came to stand beside her with his hands in the air like a surgeon waiting for gloves. "I'm ready."

"Watch me. Push with the palm of your hands into the dough, then fold to the center." She demonstrated. "Now, you try." She stepped away, allowing him space in front of the dough but stayed close.

He mimicked her actions, and must have failed because she nudged him with a hip.

"Move over and let me show you again." She went through the motions completely in the zone. "Put your hands over mine. You need to find the rhythm."

Ian moved to her side. "No, get behind me."

"Are you sure?"

"Yes. Now lay your hands over mine. Work it this way."

His movements followed hers. Her hair tickled his cheek as he peeked over her shoulder. He adjusted his head, brushing against the mass with each movement. So silky. Allison fit him perfectly from his chin to their toes. She smelled of flour, warmth, and... lavender? He inhaled. His manhood tightened.

"You push, then you fold it again. That way you're working the gluten."

Was she so innocent that she had no idea what she was doing to him? Could this go on forever? "You know I'd help bake bread all the time if I'd realized how erotic it was."

Allison's butt brushed his hard length. She sucked in a sharp breath. "I'll uh... have your lunch ready in ten minutes." She ducked under his arm. Her voice shook slightly as she asked, "Grilled cheese with your soup?"

"I'd rather have something else, but if that's all you're offering, then yes."

Allison moved across the room, stopped, and looked out the window.

Ian returned to kneading with none of his earlier interest. *Now* he was working out his frustration. He glanced over his shoulder to find Allison studying him with a perplexed expression.

Allison took a steadying breath. Her fingers still shook. Heaven help her. What had she been thinking to tell Ian to put his arms around her? She hadn't thought. As usual, her focus had been on the dough. She'd rubbed against him, of all things.

Even so, his reaction had been flattering. Looking on the bright side, it would've been worse if he hadn't had any reaction. She hmphed. Rejection she had been too familiar with. Glancing over her shoulder, she met his gaze then quickly hurried to the refrigerator. "You keep working that. It still has a few more minutes."

He grunted.

Minutes later, she called, "Your lunch is on the table. I'll take care of the dough now. You go eat before it gets cold."

"What do you want me to do with this?" He

patted the mound of dough.

She went to the other side of the table to use it as a fortress between them. There would be no more of what happened earlier. No matter how delicious it felt to have Ian desire her. She worked here. In a few weeks, she'd leave forever. She had plans, and she refused to lose sight of them regardless of her body's efforts to betray her.

Waiting until he'd stepped to the sink to wash his hands and stood well out of touching distance, she then moved to the other side of the counter.

"Aren't you going to have lunch?" Ian sounded far away, across the room, yet a shiver ran along her spine.

"I must get this in the refrigerator then go up top." She prepared the bowl as she had done the first one.

"Allison, look at me."

She didn't want to, but she couldn't think of a way to refuse him. Turning, she rested against the counter. "Yes?"

"That can wait. Join me for lunch." The pleading in his deep honeyed voice pulled at her.

Allison debated with herself. She couldn't think of a refusal that he would accept. Releasing a breath, she said, "Okay. Let me put this away."

A few minutes later, she set her bowl of soup on the table, making sure to leave an empty chair between them. He raised a brow but said nothing.

Ian picked up his spoon. "You're really into baking, aren't you?"

"I love it. It's great for stress relief." She returned to eating. The sooner she finished her meal, the quicker she could get away from Ian.

Having him show her so much interest unnerved her, especially after what had just happened between them.

"Will I be having one of your rolls this evening?"

"That's the plan."

"Good. I'm eager to try one." He picked up half of his grilled cheese sandwich and took a bite. "This is great."

"I'm glad you like it." At least she could satisfy a man in some way.

"I appreciate you pitching in to help Mrs. White. I don't have much experience in the kitchen, but if you need help."

"That's not necessary. I'll prepare plates for us and Roger if you don't care about the informal presentation." She spooned up her soup.

"That sounds fine." He'd finished his meal and sat watching her.

She picked up her napkin and wiped her mouth. "I'd think the 'lord of the manor' would have certain standards."

Ian's gaze never left hers. "You don't have a high opinion of me, do you?"

Allison concentrated on her food. "Where'd you get that idea?"

A slight smile played around his lips. "I think you're avoiding my question."

She didn't want to say what she really thought of him. It'd sound too much like a schoolgirl with a crush on the popular football player. If he knew how she felt, it would give him more power over her. Leaning forward she said, "Have you ever known me not to speak my mind?"

He barked a laugh, and his eyes twinkled with mirth. "No, I'll give you that."

"So why do you think I'd start now?" She returned to eating.

A thoughtful look came over Ian's face. "Maybe because you're attracted to me, and you're fighting it."

The man didn't lack for an ego. What made the statement irritating was that he spoke the truth.

Allison choked, jerking her napkin to her mouth. Her face heated as she stared at him. "I uh…"

He pushed out his chair, stood, and gathered his used dishes. "Thank you for my meal. I look forward to tonight's." With that, he left.

What must he think? She had been working to maintain control over her project and show her competence all the while acting like some starry-eyed besotted teen. Not like her, at all. She was too old for such behavior, and she never got personally involved with a customer. For some reason, she had lost her head where Ian was concerned.

Even if she and Ian wanted a relationship, a short affair would be the best it could be, which wouldn't be wise. Affairs didn't generally end well, and she couldn't afford any negative comments from a disgruntled lover directed toward HRD. What she needed to do was concentrate on the renovation. She groaned. But she'd told herself that since she met Ian? Yeah, and it hadn't sunk in yet.

Later that afternoon, Ian walked by the dining room and doubled back when he saw Allison with drawings strewn out on the table along with stacks of papers nearby.

"Allison?" He entered the room. So deep in

thought, she didn't even look his way as she reached across the table for a paper. "Allison, what're you doing?"

She jumped, pulling earbuds from her ears. Her back slammed against his chest. When she wobbled, his hands went to her waist to steady her. "Whoa. Careful there."

Her posterior branded him with heat. They stayed like that for a moment before reality set in. He moved, giving her space.

She faced him. "You scared me."

"I didn't mean to." He scanned the table. "What's all this?"

"I needed a wide place to spread out my detailed schematics. There's not enough space in my bedroom. Not even the bed is large enough. Mrs. White offered the dining table between meals. She told me it's the largest space available. I'll move if you'd rather I not use the space." Allison started gathering papers.

Ian placed a hand over hers stopping her movements. "You should've told me you needed a place to work or, at the very least, let Roger know. It must make for an exhausting day to have to pick up and move all these papers around all the time. Come with me."

Taking her hand he led her out of the dining room. Allison glanced at the table. "Leave everything for a minute until you return."

To his surprise, she allowed him to continue to hold her hand as they entered the foyer then made a right and headed down a hall. He stopped in front of a door, one he rarely entered, and turned the knob.

"This used to be my father's study. Was

supposed to be my brother's one day. You may use it."

The room remained dark. Heavy drapes hung over the windows. Ian remained in the doorway, but Allison slipped by him. Mrs. White had kept it as it had been when his father still lived. Well cared for and everything in its place.

Ian finally entered. "Nobody has used this room for a long time. My father and brother passed away fifteen years ago." He shook his head. "I can't believe it has been that long. In some ways, it seems like yesterday." He spoke as much to himself as to her.

"Are you sure it's okay if I use it?"

He didn't immediately answer. She faced him. "Yes, I'm sure. My father would appreciate a lovely woman using his study."

Allison flushed, then walked to the window and pulled a drape back far enough to let in a stream of light. "Wow, what a view."

Ian joined her. "You're welcome to open them all the way if you wish." He pushed the drapes wide, allowing the dim sunlight of the cloudy afternoon touch his father's belongings once again.

Allison turned to view the room. He did the same, trying to see it through her eyes. It had high arched beams and stone walls. A man-sized fireplace filled one wall. Even an oversized table that would work perfect for her drawings. She walked to the table.

"Here, you can spread out your blueprints and leave them." Ian stepped toward her.

Allison moved to one of the ceiling-high bookshelves and studied the old volumes. "Based on these, the people in your family have had interesting reading habits."

"My father read all the time. He was brilliant. I miss him every day."

She turned to him. "Will you tell me about him?"

For a moment, Ian feared he couldn't speak without choking up. "He was the kind of father who would wake us when he came home. No matter how late. He believed in duty to family as well as the business. He told me, us, my brother and sister, that the Hartley name meant something and that we must honor it. That our heritage was everything. That it was entrusted to us for the future. He lived that way."

"Do you feel the same?" She ran a finger along the spine of a book.

"I do. I'll do what's necessary to carry on the family name, and care for the land and castle."

She faced him. "Such as having the tower repaired."

"Yes, and to marry a woman who understands the need to embody the Hartley heritage, and produce an heir."

"Gezz, that sounds like a warm marriage."

He'd resigned himself, long time ago, to how his life must be. "I plan to choose wisely."

Allison nodded. "Good luck with that. Did you grow up here?"

"No, mostly in London. We came up here on holidays and school breaks. I once thought I'd make it my permanent home. Then life happened." A note of sadness circled his words.

Her gaze met his. "But you still wish you could."

"That isn't possible. My business is in London. The commute is too far. Even now, work is piling up on my desk in London."

Allison moved around the room, going to the desk and letting her fingertips trail over it. "Did you always want to follow in your father's footsteps?"

"No. That was my brother's job."

"What happened?" Allison asked softly.

"They were in Australia on a business trip and in a small engine plane accident. No one survived."

She came to him. "Oh, Ian. I'm so sorry."

"Fresh out of university, I stepped right into a job I knew little about. But I learned fast."

Allison slipped her arms around him in a tender hug. He accepted her comfort and compassion. Too soon, Allison moved away. "In seconds, it became your job to take care of the Hartley name and everything that went with that."

"Yes."

"That explains a lot. Had you planned to go into the shipping business when you finished school?"

"My degree is in countryside management. I wanted to return here and run the estate. Particularly work on innovative methods of conserving the land. Try new ways of farming. There are thousands of acres here to work."

"I hadn't expected that, but I have to admit I'm impressed."

Ian couldn't believe how much he liked her thinking highly of him. "Thanks, that was nice to hear."

She looked around the room. "I'd rather live here than in London too. Hartley Castle is a place to be proud of. Being Lord Hartley really hadn't been in your plans at all, had it?"

"No." The word came out flat even to his own ears. No point in thinking about those dreams. They're gone. Just like his father and brother.

"How difficult it must have been to give up your vision of life to take on someone else's. With all of its requirements and must-dos."

Uncomfortable with how deep their conversation had gone, Ian shifted toward the door. "Sometimes life does that to us. If you'll excuse me, I've a call to make. I'll let Mrs. White know you're going to use the study when I call to check in on her family. Feel free to make yourself at home. Move things around if you need to."

"Ian?"

He turned to her. "Yes."

"May I ask you one more question?"

His eyes narrowed. "Yes."

"Why aren't you using this as your office?"

He didn't speak right away. "I guess, in an odd way, I feel unworthy of it. I didn't want it to begin with, and then I only gained it through the death of my father and brother. Somehow it didn't seem right."

Why had he told Allison all that? He'd never told another living soul how he felt.

CHAPTER FOUR

The next morning Allison didn't see Ian as she made her way to the dining room for breakfast. The few times she'd caught a glimpse of him since she'd moved into the castle, he'd either worked at his desk or on the phone except for when he had shown her the study.

He hadn't even come to the kitchen for afternoon tea with Mrs. White. Although her granddaughter had sprained her wrist, there would be no lasting effects from the accident, and she'd returned to school the next morning. While Allison and Mrs. White chatted, the housekeeper mentioned that Ian had left early that morning.

Just when Allison's nerves had started to settle down around him, he disappeared. Their conversation in the study had made him more human and less lordly. She could see him as a hurt young man struggling with enormous loss and mammoth responsibilities. How overwhelming for him. Now she better understood his intense work ethic.

In her office once again, her phone rang. She picked it up off the desk, stopping the "Sweet Home Alabama" ring tone.

"Moore here." She listened then said, "We needed the stone delivered today as you promised. The delay could put us behind a week or more. I've masons ready to go." She paced across the colorful Oriental rug centered on the floor. "I must have that stone tomorrow, or the work will come to a halt."

How would Ian react? She didn't want him thinking she couldn't handle the contractors. He'd already been skeptical enough about that in the beginning. It had bolstered her pride when he'd been pleased with the progress upon his return from his trip. She wanted that again. It shocked her at how much his praise mattered. That he continued feeling that way mattered on a level she didn't wish to explore.

"Yes, yes, I understand. Tell your manager I'll see him in his office first thing tomorrow morning." She hung up.

Her foreman needed to know right away not to expect the stone. Allison glanced at her watch as she hurried out of the door and promptly ran into a wall of sturdy, solid chest. The hardhat in her hand fell to the floor, rattling to a stop.

Long fingers cupped her shoulders, steadying her. *Ian.* His aftershave gave him away. It reminded her of a freshly cut lemon. Her blood pressure skyrocketed twenty points. She savored the pleasant aroma and controlled her urge to inhale deeply.

"Hey, are you all right?"

"Yeah." She stepped out of his reach.

"As much as I enjoy having a woman throw herself into my arms, I don't usually have them barreling into me." The humor in his voice both surprised her and made her gooey at the same time. "I do hope you're more careful when you're climbing around up top. I've already had to save you once."

Afraid that her face had turned as red as her hair, Allison refused to meet his eyes. She focused on the center of his chest. "I can assure you I'm usually very surefooted."

Ian chuckled. "What're you saying? That I make you weak-kneed?"

She couldn't tell him the truth. "Mrs. White said you weren't here."

"I couldn't stay away." The air between them grew charged.

"Sweet Home Alabama" interrupted them. She stepped further away before answering the phone. "Let me call you back."

Ian raised his aristocratic brow. "What kind of ring tone is that?"

She gave him a cheeky smile. "A little touch of home."

"You certainly don't have any trouble knowing when a call is yours." He didn't sound impressed with her choice of songs. "I'd like a tour of the construction area."

"Is that you asking or telling?" Most of her clients, despite being rich or famous, at least asked.

He dipped his chin. "Excuse me. Would you please give me a tour?"

"Much nicer, thank you."

Ian took a step closer, almost into her personal

space. Her entire body went on alert. "I don't often let people correct me."

Allison had no doubt. "When would you like that tour?"

His gaze intensified for a moment. Were they talking about the same thing?

"Now's good with me. Just let me change." He left the room.

Dressed in one of his impeccably cut suits, he looked like the epitome of the billionaire shipping magnate. His dress said power, but she liked him best in his casual clothes that screamed sex appeal. His worn jeans and the dark cable sweater that brought out the stormy blue of his eyes was her favorite. She hoped he didn't wear that outfit, because she might lose her footing and fall for real.

Allison huffed. How would the obituary read? "Killed by a blue sweater and to-die-for-eyes."

Fifteen minutes later, Ian accepted the white hardhat that Allison offered him from the rack sitting outside the tower stairwell. The men had left to have their tea break—something always important for a crew.

He tossed the hat between his hands, examining it.

"Don't even think about going any farther unless you wear the helmet." Allison's voice held a note of authority. "On my jobs, safety comes first."

The corner of his mouth lifted. She'd guessed what he'd had in mind. He hadn't planned to wear it. After all, he'd climbed to the top of the tower all his life. Instead of ruffling her feathers, he chose to place the hat on his head.

She turned and stepped with sure feet over the boarded catwalk lying across the roof to the wall of the tower. He followed her pink-hatted head and tight-jeaned bottom. The view so enticing. For some reason he didn't quite understand, Allison fascinated him. She was pretty enough, yet he knew women more beautiful. Her intelligence was impressive, but he'd never found that necessary before in a woman. Could the appeal be that she wasn't intimidated by him? Whatever the reason, the attraction hummed like a live wire between them.

Ian took pride in remaining in control of himself and his world. Allison made him fear losing his grip. He shook his head, bringing his thoughts back to what she said.

"One of our struggles is to adhere to historical reconstruction guidelines. Finding matching local stone can be difficult. There's not always enough being quarried when it's needed." She looked at him. "Our work must match the original as close as possible. Sometimes that means removing some stones before rebuilding."

He liked the fact that she had used the word our when referring to the project. In his business, he understood employees worked better when they felt ownership. He encouraged that in his own company, in an effort to create a successful environment, both for the employee and the company. He also appreciated the passionate way Allison spoke about her work. Maybe they were more alike than he'd given her credit for.

She glanced at him. The soft breeze blew her russet hair across her cheek. He came close to groaning out loud. Couldn't she control that glorious mass? Unable to resist, he reached up and wrapped the corkscrew length of silk around his finger.

Allison blinked twice, fast.

Ian pulled his finger out of the long curl. "You have the most amazing hair."

"Uh...thank you. Let's...uh go this way." She moved to a ladder standing against the tower wall. He noticed her hand shaking as she gripped the metal.

Ian couldn't help the swell of male pride. Allison wasn't completely unaffected by him either. He felt the magnetism. And he wanted her to feel it as well.

She waved her hand in the direction of the other three towers that made up the corners of the castle. "The steps are being reconstructed. You'll have to come up this way."

"I didn't realize this amount of detail went into a renovation."

"It's my job to see that there's as little distinguishable difference between old and new." This time confidence filled her voice. "Please follow me, and I'll show you what we've completed."

How had he ever thought Allison might fall from the wall? She was too self-assured and self-reliant. Everything about her screamed she could take care of herself. The exact opposite of the women he normally dated. His ex-wife, a case in point. She'd needed attention constantly.

The view of Allison's slim hips swaying as she moved up the aluminum ladder with the grace of a lioness made his body stiffen. He'd better get his thoughts on what he was doing, or he might have a mishap.

"Let me get off the ladder before you start up," she called from above. She moved away. "Okay. Your turn."

Ian started his climb. Stepping off the ladder, he met Allison's amused grin.

"I thought for a minute there, you might be afraid of heights."

"No. I'll do almost anything when there's a beautiful woman waiting for me."

Allison's blush made the freckles bridging her nose more prominent. Ian tapped the end of it with his forefinger. "Even cuter." He chuckled when her blush deepened.

She turned quickly and moved toward the outside wall. "Why're you flirting with me?"

He grinned, watching her closely. "Why wouldn't I flirt with you?"

"Because you are 'Lord Hartley' and I'm not of your social set. I suspect you're teasing me."

"Maybe a little but I find I like you. And I'm a man, after all, and you are an attractive woman."

"You could get in trouble saying things like that with me working for you."

Ian gave her a sly smile. "Are you going to tell on me? I can assure you I don't normally speak to women in my employ this way, but with you, I can't help myself. I find you fascinating. And I think you feel the same about me."

Allison's eyes widened as if she hadn't expected that statement. "Don't."

"Flirt or find you fascinating?"

She gave him an earnest look. "Both. Now, come this way, but watch your step."

Ian maneuvered around piles of stones and tools. Joining her, he kept his distance as he stared across the rock-strewn fields. The afternoon sun warmed his face as he watched the sheep meandering as they grazed. The copse of trees further beyond them had been his favorite playground as a boy. "Much too long since I've taken the time to come up here."

"It's an amazing view. I come up almost every evening. Great place to think." She bit her lip.

Had she let a secret slip? "You do? Any chance I might get an invitation to join you sometime?"

She shrugged her shoulders. "It's your castle. I guess you can come and go as you please."

"I can, but..." He stooped to see under the brim of her hat, meeting her gaze. "It would be so much nicer to be invited."

She continued to watch him. "You're doing it again."

Why did she so badly want to keeping him at arms' length? He found her attractive, and he knew well when a woman felt the same about him. Maybe she was right, and it was a bad idea. His interest might be unprofessional, but he couldn't help himself.

"Let me show you this area we're working on." Allison pointed to the stone. "We'll have to support it to the left before doing more masonry work. It'll take about a week to accomplish that."

One corner of the tower remained intact, while the other three were in various degrees of deconstruction. Scaffolding surrounded the outside wall corner.

"What's happening on the outside wall?"

"We had to reinforce it with iron bars. Iron rods are also being run through certain stones to ensure stability. There's an art to placing the stone. I have the best artisans. By the end of next week, this area should be stable enough for you to enter the rooms inside the tower."

Ian ran his hand over the rock his ancestors had placed on the wall of the castle. "Despite my initial concern, I'm impressed with your knowledge and progress."

A huge grin covered her lips. Allison glowed under his praise. She made a small bow of her head. "Why, thank you, Lord Hartley."

Had she thought about curtseying as well? He now knew how to please her. She took pride in her work.

Ian scanned the area. "I thought the stone was to be delivered by now."

Her smile faded, replaced by a solemn look. "Yes, I'm having some difficulty getting it. I spoke to the quarry this afternoon. They're saying a week's delay. I'm driving over to Stillshire tomorrow to discuss it with the quarry owner. I've used this company before on other projects and have never had this problem."

"They gave you no indication of why they can't deliver?"

"No, but I'll work it out." She met his gaze. Her voice took on a firm note. "I'll handle the problem."

"I've no doubt you're capable, but would you mind if I go along with you tomorrow?" The question popped out before he realized it. He didn't have time for such.

Allison opened her mouth, and he stopped her with a raised hand. "I have no intention of interfering. I won't even flirt if you insist. I'd just like to have a day away from work. And I know a nice little pub near there that serves great fish and chips." He applied his winning smile. Something about spending the morning getting to know Allison better tempted to him.

She opened and closed her mouth and opened it again in an obvious debate with herself about how to respond. If it wouldn't have hurt her feelings, he would've laughed.

"If you really think you'd like to go. I guess the company would be nice." Her lack of enthusiasm with the idea boarded on comical.

Stepping into her personal space enough she had to tilt her head to meet his gaze, he said in a teasing voice, "You know Allison, you could bruise my ego with the lack of interest you show at the thought of spending time with me." Gently, he tugged on the same escaped curl. "I promise my best behavior."

She watched him intently for a moment before she stepped away. Her hair slowly left his fingers. "I'm leaving at seven in the morning if you want to go."

"I'll meet you in the great hall."

The next morning Ian stood waiting on Allison in the great hall. She arrived right on time.

She reminded him of a cherub with her creamy skin and scattering of pale strawberry freckles. Her mass of red curls gave her a sizzling halo. Secured on the sides with whips of hair feathering her forehead and cheeks, she looked younger than her years. For the meeting, she'd dressed in the same gray suit she'd wore the day they met, but this time a pale pink top peeked out from underneath.

"Good morning."

"Mornin'" She stepped up beside him.

"I thought we'd stop in the village for breakfast and told Mrs. White not to worry about lunch."

"Okay." Allison headed toward the door.

"By the way, I'm going to drive. You scare me."

Allison grinned over her shoulder. "Suits me."

A light mist fell and fog hung low over the rolling hills as Ian drove away from the castle. In the village, he pulled to a stop in front of the bakery. A small bell tinkled as they entered.

"Good day, Allison. Ian." The middle-aged woman said from behind the glass case that held pastries of every size and shape.

"Hi, Nellie. How've you been?" Allison peered into the case.

"Hello, Nellie," Ian joined as he gave Allison a curious glance. She recognized Nellie?

"Just fine. What can I get you two?" She reached for a wax paper from a box.

"I'll have my usual cheese Danish, please." Allison pulled napkins from a dispenser.

"I'll have the same and a coffee." Ian turned to Allison. "Anything to drink?"

"Oh, ah, and tea."

Ian pursed his lips, and made a little nod before saying with a grin, "Hot tea? Interesting. For the queen of iced tea."

"I'm not completely set in my ways." One side of Allison's lips moved upward.

"That's useful to know." He handed Nellie the money.

As she placed their choices in a white paper bag, Ian glanced from Nellie to Allison. "So how did you and Nellie meet?"

"She used to stop by most mornings." Nellie handed Ian the bag and change.

"Yeah, bakeries are great places to meet people when you're new in town. Shouldn't we get going?"

"We should."

Allison sat beside him eating her pastry. She brushed the crumbs off her chest. Maybe he should've let her drive. She wasn't making it easy for him to do so safely. With her housekeeping done, she settled into the seat.

"How far is it to Stillshire?"

"Almost an hour away." He concentrated as he entered a roundabout.

"That's not as far as I feared. You know, this is a beautiful country. I envy you living here."

Ian glanced at her. Allison peered out the window with a dreamy expression on her face.

"You wouldn't so much in the winter. It can be bitter cold then. It's difficult to keep the castle warm. I've often wondered how my ancestors survived. I can't imagine wearing enough furs to ever be comfortable."

She laughed. "I bet they spent most of their time by a fire."

"Tell me about your home?"

"I don't really have one." A sad note crept in her voice.

"Why?"

"My father is career military. We lived all over the world. Never stayed in one place long."

"That's why you learned to drive in Italy."

Allison smiled. "Yeah. We always lived on base. I lived in a dorm in college. Then I had jobs all over the place and stayed in hotels. I don't even have a rented apartment to go home to." She sighed. "But I'll soon have my grandparents' house."

She spoke more to herself than him.

"You're looking forward to that, aren't you?"

"I am. I'm so tired of living out of a suitcase. I want to sleep in my own bed for a change." Her words softly trailed out.

"I know what you mean. I travel too much, but it's necessary if I want to keep Hartley Shipping going."

Her attention hadn't strayed from the scenery. "At least you have Hartley Castle to come home to."

"I do. I just wish I had more time to spend here."

"If it were mine, I'd make sure to." She didn't say it as a reprimand but more as a statement.

"Do you have someone special you plan to share your house with?"

She glared at him. "Are you asking if I have a boyfriend, Lord Hartley?"

"I could be."

"Not anymore."

"Do you mind telling me what happened?"

"Let's just say I didn't meet his requirements."

Something about the way Allison said those words made him believe she'd been deeply hurt. Ian didn't like that idea.

"Tell me about these partners of yours. Are they good with you becoming COO instead of toiling in the field?"

"Oh yeah. They want me to be happy. They support what I've worked toward for years."

"Won't you miss hands-on work?"

"I plan to continue working on special projects. Also small jobs in the States. I'm not giving restoration up completely."

"How did you and your partners get together?"

"You're sure full of questions."

Ian shrugged. "Just making conversation."

"I've never thought of you a conversationalist for the heck of it."

He took his eyes off the road long enough to see her suspicious look. "I promise there's no hidden agenda here. Just interested."

"Okay. We met in college. I'd lived all over, and Mallory and Jordon came from the opposite ends of the country. It's Mallory Andrews and Jordon Glass. You might know Mallory. She did some modeling at one time."

"And you're assuming that I know all the models?"

"Well, the magazines say you like them."

He smirked. "Don't trust everything you read. And *no,* I don't believe I've met Ms. Andrews."

"Touché."

"Please go on." He used his boardroom tone.

She chuckled. "Anyway, we had a class together. Formed a study group and bonded over our fascination with old buildings. After graduation, we went our separate ways but kept in touch. During a girls' weekend, we were commiserating about how much we'd like to work for ourselves. So, we decided to take a chance and start our own company. We each brought special skills and knowledge to form a well-rounded niche company. Now you have our story."

"Now you're planning to change things up a bit?"

"I am. And looking forward to it." A happy, eager note lifted her voice.

How long had it been since he had felt the same way? He was locked into Hartley Shipping forever. He shifted into the next roundabout and smoothly shifted up again, giving the powerful car more gas than necessary, sending them flying along the road.

"How much longer?"

"Ten minutes."

"Good. I'm ready to get this over with." She pulled out some papers and began shuffling through them.

"Are you expecting a scene?"

"Not really. But you never know how some people will react to me." She gave him a direct glance.

"Point taken."

Allison, with Ian following, entered Welche's office less than half an hour later. Allison made the introductions between the men.

Ian shook hands with the short, barrel-chested man before they all took a seat.

"Lord Hartley. I hadn't expected to see you." The quarry manager's voice went a little higher.

"I'm interested in where my stone is coming from. The castle's very important to our family. Ms.

Moore is kind enough to let me tag along."

"Well, how can I help you?" Mr. Welche focused on Ian.

Allison scooted to the edge of her chair, drawing the man's attention. "Mr. Welche, you know exactly how you can help. I need the stone I ordered over two weeks ago delivered. I spoke to your special project manager and was assured that your company could handle my order. For some reason, it's now delayed."

"Ms. Moore," his tone sounding placating, "I understand your frustration, but we're doing the best we can. We've had machinery go down and some personal issues."

Allison leaned forward. "I can appreciate having issues, but I still need that stone. I've a job to complete, and you promised stone. You've missed two delivery times with no explanation of why, or reaching out to us first."

"We've other shipments that are on backorder. Please understand." His voice had turned pleading.

"Mr. Welche, we've had a good relationship in the past. I'd prefer not to have to take my business elsewhere, but I will if I must. You need to understand that we're not talking about this project only, but projects in the future as well. You'll lose all of HRD business." She emphasized the last words.

Mr. Welche paled under his ruddy complexion. "Now Ms. Moore, I don't think it will come to that. Surely we can work something out."

"I hope so, but if you don't come through with at least a partial shipment by the middle of next week, I'll have no choice but to go to one of your competitors."

The man circled the desk facing Allison. "Ms. Moore, I'd like to keep your business. I'll do what I can to make that happen."

"I'd like that too. Keep me in the loop and have the stone delivered when scheduled." Allison came to her feet, and Ian stood. She sensed him moving closer. Was he afraid Mr. Welche might threaten her? She didn't think that would happen but she liked having Ian nearby. "Please honor our original agreement, and I'll be happy."

The man took a moment before he spoke. "I'll discuss the problem again with my plant manager and see what we can do. I'll even consider putting on a second shift. But no promises."

"It sounds like those aren't any good anyway," Ian muttered.

Allison gave him a quelling look, before turning to Mr. Welche. "Thank you."

She then stepped around her chair and walked to the door with head held high and her shoulders back. She didn't wait on Ian to follow, not slowing until she reached the car. She took a couple of cleansing breaths while she waited for Ian to join her. Her hands shook, and her jaw hurt from clenching it.

A large hand slid over her back like a comforting blanket on a freezing day and came to rest on her shoulder. "When my negotiations aren't going well, I'm going to call on you," Ian said, his mouth close enough that his words ruffled her hair. "Impressive, Ms. Moore."

"I hate those *kinds* of meetings. But sometimes it's the only way to get the supplier to take me seriously."

He made a low chuckle. "I believe this one

does. *Now.*"

Allison turned to him. Ian's hand fell to his side. She missed its reassuring weight. "I'm really glad you were there. It was nice to have you standing beside me. That could've turned ugly."

He gave her a wry smile and nodded. "I think it's time for us to find that pub."

Half an hour later, Allison sat across the wooden table from Ian in the pub booth. They waited on their order. She swirled her straw around in her cola. It had been nice to have him along. Her ex would have said she'd overreacted. That she always had to prove herself.

She needed time to let her annoyance ease. Ian didn't force a conversation. To her surprise, the silence felt relaxed like two people comfortable with each other. A couple of days ago she hadn't thought that possible.

Their food arrived.

Allison said as the man who brought their food walked away, "Since I need some downtime to decompress, it's your turn to talk."

"Talk?" Ian made it sound like a terrifying idea.

She grinned. "Easy. I'm not going to make you reveal state secrets."

"Okay. I don't make a habit of doing either."

"I kind of figured that." She took a bite of her fish.

"What do you want to know?"

"Anything. How about telling me about your family?"

"I've spoken about my father. William, my older brother, loved to laugh but could be a tough businessman. He would have done great things with Hartley Shipping if he had lived."

Did Ian think he hadn't?

"Mum is Mum and then some. She and Dad had a great marriage, and she has searched for another one in all the wrong places with all the wrong men."

Allison reached over and touched his arm. "I'm sorry."

"I don't like it, but I have to remind myself she's an adult. I just have to live with it and keep her bank account full." He paused. "Bloody hell. I shouldn't have said anything like that. I've a good mother. She loves me. What I should've said is she's flamboyant and the life of the party."

"She sounds like a fun person."

"She is. You'd like her. Everyone does." A wispy note crept into his voice.

"And you love her?"

His gaze met hers. "She drives me crazy, but I do. Very much."

"I think we all have someone in our life who does that."

Ian took a swallow of his drink. "Who's yours?"

"I'd have to say my father. He put a lot of pressure on us kids to be the best, to succeed. It's because of him I'm an engineer."

"Really?" Ian watched her with interest.

"He was an engineer, my grandfather was an engineer, and Dad wanted one of us kids to be an engineer. I was the best at math, so I won."

"I'm just guessing, but not your first choice."

"I love my job, but I would've liked to have had a choice."

"What would you do then?"

"I'd own a bakery."

He grinned. "Why am I not surprised?"

"I thought we were supposed to talk about you. Didn't I hear something about you having a sister?"

"Yes, Clarissa. She's divorced and has two children. They're great. She'll visit for school break. I'm hoping you'll be done before she gets here."

Allison could hear the love Ian felt for his family. "If I can get that stone, we have a better chance of that happening. A construction area doesn't make for a good playground for children."

"No, it doesn't. I think she wants to show her kids the good times she had at Hartley Castle. She's trying to get her life together since the divorce."

She looked at him for a moment. "So, how about you? Ever tried marriage?"

That subject Ian didn't wish to discuss. It hadn't been his finest hour. In many ways, his weakest. "Once. Not for long. Soon after my father and brother died."

"I imagine you didn't take the breakup well."

"I don't do failure well. Turns out a good Lady Hartley needs more than the right breeding. She liked the title better than she liked me." It still hurt that Judith had used him so.

"Is that so?"

Ian started to refuse to say more but for some reason he wanted her to know. "Our families knew each other. Everyone believed we were the perfect match. Only thing is she didn't love me, and I had too little time for her while trying to understand the estate and rebuild the company. She went elsewhere for attention. With more than one man." To his ears, he sounded pathetic.

Allison placed her hand over his for a moment. "I'm sorry that happened to you. No one deserves that kind of treatment."

"To say I don't have much interest in another marriage would be an understatement. Still, I have the responsibility to provide an heir." Even to himself, he sounded more resigned to the idea instead of happy about fathering a child.

"Continuing the Hartley name's important?"

"Yes. It's been drummed into me since birth. I also want to honor my father and brother. My nephew's my heir, but I'd like to keep our family name going. There's also a position in Parliament to consider."

"Understandable. That's a heavy burden to carry, I imagine. Living up to everyone else's expectations. I'm glad I don't have to live under that pressure." She wrinkled up her nose and shook her head. "I don't think I'd do well under such demands. I don't much like being told what to do."

Ian looked at her and grinned. "Is that so?" Time to move away from this pathetic subject. "If you didn't need to return right away, I thought you might enjoy going to the village market."

Allison smiled. "That's the last thing I expected you to suggest. I assumed you'd have to hurry back for work. I never assumed Lord Hartley would enjoy a market, but I'd love to go."

He shrugged. "You make 'Lord Hartley' sound like a dirty word. I'm human too. I told you I need a little time off. I've not visited a market in years. Haven't had the time."

"Walking's a great way to get some exercise

before we get in the car."

His voice dipped low. "I could think of other ways to do that."

Pink formed on her cheeks. "Ian, you promised."

"I did." He threw his napkin on the table and cleared his throat. "Ready?"

"Sure."

They ambled through the narrow city streets to the center of town and the village green. People mingled around tables lining the sidewalks creating the weekly market area.

"When I was young, and we stayed at the castle, my family went to the village market regularly. My father adored people." Ian stepped around a child chasing a ball.

"Where I'm from, we call them flea markets. My father wouldn't step foot in one." Allison laughed. "But this market's more upscale than ours."

"Here, it isn't just about finding a bargain, but also a social event. That's what my father enjoyed. Meeting the people of our village."

She placed her hand on his arm. "It sounds like you had a wonderful father."

He took her hand and held it as they continued to walk.

"I did. He worked hard, but he always had time for his family." He tugged her hand. "Come this way. Let's see what's further along the street."

They moved between the booths.

"Hey, look." She let go of his fingers and headed toward a table filled with antique kitchen utensils. Searching through the silver-colored items, she picked up one and examined it, before finding another, then digging through the pile again. Some of the gadgets had rusted and had obvious signs of extensive use.

He had been completely forgotten as she explored. Allison's eyes sparkled, and she almost shook with excitement. If this amount of interest had been directed toward another man, he would've been jealous.

"Oh my, look at this." Her voice held a breathless quality. She acted like a kid who had found a missing toy.

Ian couldn't help but be captivated by her excitement. He chuckled. "What is it?"

She gave him a disbelieving look. His smile grew.

"It's a pastry cutter," she said, as if he should have known that.

"Oh. I can't imagine how I didn't see that."

She returned to sorting through the stuff again.

"This is great, too." She'd picked up something and turned it one way then another. Ian had no idea its purpose and he didn't plan to ask. Instead, he leaned his hip against the pole, and crossed his arms.

"I'm going to have to get this." She handed money to the man.

Allison's smile reminded him of the thrill he got after making a particularly difficult business deal come together.

Allison had no poker face. What she felt shown bright. She'd found the greatest treasure. The woman who had made her demands to the quarry manager and the one Ian saw now were two different women.

She lifted her purchases high. "I can hardly wait to use this."

Ian gave her an incredulous glance. "Use it? To do what?"

Her shocked expression made him laughed. Something he'd not done in a long time.

"Why, to cut butter into flour when I'm making pie crusts or biscuits." She spoke as if he were the village simpleton.

"I see." He nodded as if giving the idea a thoughtful response.

Allison brought a hand to her hip, her smile growing until it spread across her face. "You've no idea what I'm talking about, do you?"

He pursed his lips, and then shrugged, "None."

"Imagine the great Lord Hartley doesn't know everything."

"You're doing it again."

Her tone teased, and her eyes turned a deeper green. She turned thoughtful for a moment. "Maybe I should teach you how to use it sometime."

"If it's anything like last time, sign me up for a lesson." Ian made the words sound suggestive on purpose. He earned the reward of Allison's gasp and deep blush before she walked away.

With a smile on his face, he caught up with her. They strolled back the way they'd come. Allison stopped often to browse at a booth, and he waited patiently, surprising himself. Patience had never been one of his finer points, but he found he enjoyed watching Allison. He liked her too much.

Finally, he said, "I think we'd better leave for home." *Home.* He'd not thought of Hartley Castle as home in a long time. He had spent little time there in recent years, since taking over Hartley Shipping.

"I know." Regret filled her voice. "But I appreciate you letting me have a chance to blow off some steam."

"You're welcome. We'll have to go to the market in Hartshire one day soon."

She smiled. "That sounds like fun."

The desire to pick her up and kiss her shot through him. A man bumping his shoulder brought him to his senses. "I do have a late conference call this afternoon, so we should be on our way."

"You're always expecting a call or leaving on some trip." Her eyes widened before she looked away. "I'm sorry. I shouldn't have said that."

His hand rested lightly at her small of her back as he guided her through the crowd. "I do, don't I. For years, I've had to work 24/7. Now I don't know how to stop."

"Then today's a good time to start. I try to take time between jobs. I hope to see my partners for some much-needed beach time soon."

"That sounds like the right way to live. I need to take some lessons from you."

When they arrived at the castle an hour later, Allison scooted out of his car. "I need to talk to my foreman. Tell him to expect some stone." She gave him a shy smile. Which completely disarmed him being so unlike her. "Thanks for your support today. Glad you were there."

To say that must have been a major concession for Allison. He walked around the front of the car to stand beside her. "I'm glad I went as well."

Despite his promise, he couldn't help but brush a wayward strand of hair away from her mouth. His finger lingered at the V. She opened her mouth slightly, catching the tip. A soft sound of contentment escaped her lips. His mind ran to thoughts of kissing that same spot and hearing her purr in his ear.

Removing his finger, he trailed it lightly over her cheek. "I had a nice time."

She watched him. His gaze moved to her lips. Her tongue peeked out.

That simple move undid him. He lowered his mouth to hers, finding the warm, cushy bed of her lips. They were everything he had anticipated. As he applied more pressure, Allison joined in the kiss. Heat shot through him. His hands went to her waist to pull her closer. Just as he started to take the kiss even deeper, she broke away, turned, and headed toward the door of the castle.

"Allison," he called.

"What?" She turned, the word coming out as little more than an absent-minded whisper.

"Your baking thing." He held it up.

"Oh." This time she sounded disappointed.

Ian took one of her hands, turned it over, and cradled it before placing the gadget in her fingers.

She grasped her pastry cutter and hurried inside.

After dinner that evening, Allison sat in Ian's father's study, which she now considered her office, for her weekly video conference with Mallory and Jordon. She missed her friends. Often their calls were the highlight of her week.

She had hardly been able to eat her dinner with Ian and Roger. She kept remembering how Ian kissed her. She stared at his mouth. More than once, she hadn't responded to a question. No longer a schoolgirl, she shouldn't act so giddy about a simple kiss. It meant nothing. He probably didn't think anything of it. While his lips moving over hers replayed over and over in her mind.

"Allison, where did you go?" Mallory asked.

In the middle of their business meeting, Allison blinked. She'd half listened, "I'm listening."

"It doesn't seem that way." Mallory studied her.

Jordon stated, "I should finish with this project soon and be ready to move on to the one near York soon. Maybe we can see each other for real."

Mallory groaned. "I'm stuck on this hotel redecorating project for months to come. Maybe you two could come see me. At least we'd all be in the same area for a change."

Allison would love to see them both.

"Let's try to make that happen," Allison said. "Jordon, isn't your next project the one for the baron who wants an entire wing modernized?"

"That's the one. The baron and his daughter live there. I'll have to work around them."

Jordon had had a horrible experience in college and kept all men at arm's length because of it. The fact she agreed to work with a live-in client around would be difficult for her. From the tone of her voice, she wasn't looking forward to dealing with a man underfoot all the time. Allison could sympathize on a different level after working with Ian in residence.

"Now's yours going, Al? The *lord of the manor* still giving you a hard time?" Mallory asked.

In more ways than one. Allison's cheeks heated with thoughts of hers and Ian's kiss. "Yeah, you could say that."

Jordon demanded. "What's that blush for? Has he done something inappropriate? Be careful, Al."

Mallory leaned closer to her screen. "Hey, your cheeks are red. What *has* happened?"

"Nothing. Just a friendly kiss."

"Aw, Al, with his reputation, you need to be careful," Jordon said.

Her reaction saddened Allison. She hated Jordon's wariness. She'd make a great wife and mother with her understanding heart and furiously protective ways. "I'm watching myself. I promise. We spent the day together, and he said goodbye. It was no big deal."

Mallory giggled. "You sly dog. You kissed Lord Hartley. Women worldwide are green with envy."

"I didn't plan it!" Allison shrieked. She looked at the door, hoping Ian hadn't walked by at that moment.

"It doesn't matter. At least you noticed something hot-blooded instead of a pile of flour!" Mallory returned.

"I'm not that bad, am I?" Had she become so lost in anger over how Dan had treated her that she'd shut men out? "Would you believe Ian out and out accused me of being attracted to him?"

"Allison, you need to be careful." Jordon's face turned serious.

"So, what did you say?" Mallory's eyes were wide with anticipation of Allison's answer.

"Nothing. What could I say?"

"That you're not attracted to him," Jordon suggested.

Mallory focused on Allison. "But that's not true, is it?"

Allison shrugged. "I found him irritating when I first got here. But he really can be charming. And sort of sad too. He lost his father and older brother in the same plane accident, making him an earl and head of Hartley Shipping far too young."

"That is sad," Jordon said.

"Hey, my phone's ringing. I'm expecting a call about a shipment. I gotta go. Keep us posted on the hunky lord." Mallory's face disappeared.

"Don't do anything you'll live to regret, Al." Jordon's gloomy eyes made Allison want to reach through the screen and hug her.

"Jordon, you do know all men aren't bad?"

"That's what they say. Call me if you need me. I'll come running."

Allison had no doubt she would. "My heart's in no danger."

"That's what they all say just before that traitorous organ gets captured." The screen went black.

Was her heart in danger? No. Nothing like that.

Allison closed her eyes. In many ways, this week came close to perfect. She'd spent time baking in a wonderful kitchen, working at a job she loved, had visited with her best friends, and spent a day with a man who interested her and given her a kiss to savor. A week to remember and the kind of life she'd dreamed of.

CHAPTER FIVE

Allison entered her bedroom the next afternoon. The day had proved impossible. She had done little more than put out fires the entire time. Frustration had settled into a pain between her shoulder blades. She needed that stone here yesterday. If some of it didn't arrive soon, she'd have to go searching elsewhere. That'd mean more work and time. Without the stone, the masons couldn't start on the turrets.

Right now, she planned to take a moment to clear her head. She sat on the bed and unlaced her boots to put on her tennis shoes. Glancing out the long narrow window, she decided there was enough daylight for her to get a quick walk in before dark. She would eat dinner later since Mrs. White had the night off.

It wasn't difficult to make it out of the castle without being seen. She headed down the drive, turned up the winding and narrow road that led away from the village. Moving along at a steady pace she decided to forgo power walking and enjoy a nice peaceful stroll in the countryside.

Allison inhaled the sweet, damp air from the rain that afternoon. Raising her hands above her head in pleasure, she took a good stretch. Releasing a breath, her arms fell to her sides before she turned in a circle. She enjoyed the view of the lush green fields and craggy dips in the landscape. A rise in the road allowed her to look across the fields crisscrossed by stone fences. Just ahead, a farmer herded sheep.

"May I help you?" she asked the old man holding a staff.

"Aye," he told her, along with some other words so thick she could hardly understand.

Allison put out her hands and made a shushing sound encouraging the animals through a gate. She made good progress until one sly lamb became separated from its mother who had already gone through the gate.

Allison bent, reaching for the lamb, but it scurried away. She went after it again, and this time she captured it—but not before she sprawled across the grass.

A chuckle came from above. She looked up, expecting the sound to have come from the old man. Instead, she found Ian. Where had he come from?

"Allison, you hold on to the yearling, and I'll help you up." He allowed her no time to respond before both hands came to her waist. She pulled the lamb into her arms as Ian lifted her. He held her steady while she got her feet under her.

Ian wrapped one arm securely around her waist. His hair tickled her right ear as Ian helped her hold the lamb when it kicked. She liked being against Ian.

"Here, give him to me before he hurts you." Ian stepped around her and reached for the animal.

The lamb flexed in resistance but settled into Ian's arms without squirming further when he spoke in a quiet voice next to its ear. He walked over to the gate and sat the animal on its feet. It scampered off to join its mother.

Ian waved her close then spoke to the older gentleman standing beside him.

Allison dusted the grass and dirt from her clothes before she joined the two men.

"Allison, I'd like you to meet Mr. McGregor."

She suppressed the laugh that begged to escape. Farmer McGregor. Her mother had read all the Beatrix Potter's stories to her when she was a child. At least the man had sheep trouble not rabbit. "Hello, Mr. McGregor."

"Hi, gal. You look no worse for wear, now." He wore a broad grin. "Wee lamb can be a handful."

Allison returned his smile.

"As a boy, I spent all my spare time at Hartley Castle following Mr. McGregor. He even let me muck out the barn. He made it sound like a great honor to clean out the manure. I'd no idea at the time it was the most detested job on the farm."

The man gave her a toothy smile. "Aye, the lad did a grand job of it."

Allison grinned, not because Ian had been conned, but because Mr. McGregor had called him a lad. She couldn't imagine the structured, all-business Ian as a boy in big rubber boots using a shovel.

Ian grinned. "I know now I was having my leg pulled, but at the time, I was a boy with an important job."

Allison smiled. She liked this side of Ian. The lines on his face were not ones of tiredness and worry or worse, but of more carefree days.

"Mrs. McGregor would have you come for dinner." The words were more statement than invitation.

"That sounds grand," Ian said.

"I'll head back to the castle. Nice to meet you, Mr. McGregor." Allison stepped away.

"Miss, you're welcome as well," Mr. McGregor said.

She glanced at Ian.

Ian's look issued a dare. "One of Mrs. McGregor's meals isn't to be missed."

"Okay." Allison's attention returned to Mr. McGregor. "Thank you, that sounds nice." She spotted Ian's grin.

The three of them walked through two more fields into a farmyard with a stone house and a large barn off to the side. Everything appeared in perfect order.

Mrs. McGregor embraced Ian as if he were a long-lost son. Allison could see the true affection between them. Seconds later, she sank into Mrs. McGregor's ample embrace as well. Her generous smile and the spots of red on her cheeks assured Allison she had found a new friend. She liked Mrs. McGregor instantly.

Wood and stone walls, gleaming counters from years of use, and a flagstone floor with a stove off to one side. A large round table sat in the middle of the room, and in the center rested a platter filled with a hearty meal of meat and potatoes. The farmhouse enveloped them into the warm arms of a mother on a cold night. The type of place she wanted.

"I saw you acomin'. Sit here," she indicated a chair. "Ian, you know which seat is ours."

He'd visited the McGregor's enough that he had his own place at the table. Ian had been born with a silver spoon, yet he understood what working with his hands meant. He didn't think himself above these hardworking people. There was more to Ian than she had given him credit for.

The meal contained lively conversation between Ian and the McGregors as they caught up on each other's lives. Allison enjoyed the older couple. A few times, she and Ian exchanged a look, grinning over something said. What would it be like to have this type of evening anytime she wanted?

With the food eaten, Mr. McGregor pushed away from the table, put his hand over his stomach, winked at his wife, and said, "I've a wee repair on a stall gate I must do."

"I'll help," Ian said, standing. "You don't mind staying a bit longer, do you, Allison?"

For someone unsure about spending time with Ian, she shouldn't remain. "I can find my own way home."

Ian gave her a concerned look. "I can't let you do that."

And she couldn't let him not help when his strength might be needed by Mr. McGregor. "I'll wait. I'll help Mrs. McGregor clean up while you're busy."

"You don't have to do that. But I would enjoy

your company." Mrs. McGregor stood and picked up a bowl.

Allison waved Ian off with Mr. McGregor and stacked the dishes.

"So, you're working for Ian?" Mrs. McGregor sounded as if she were fishing for information.

"Yes, I'm overseeing the repair on the castle tower." Allison crossed the room to the sink.

Mrs. McGregor made a clicking sound. "You're not Ian's usual type."

Allison's cheeks heated. "I only work for Ian. Nothing more."

She picked up the empty platter. "Yes, but he's never brought a woman here before."

Allison made no comment and began washing a plate.

"You know," Mrs. McGregor continued, "Ian was such a happy child. When his family came for holidays, we're the first place he would visit. Our son Rob and Ian used to play together and were such great pals. But then his father and brother died. So sad. It changed Ian. He has much on his shoulders. His mother is lonely, and she worries Ian. He does the same over his sister. Then that awful wife of his... He has a hard time remembering when all was right with his world. Tis good to see him smiling. I think you are good for him."

"Mrs. McGregor..."

The door opened with a stomping of heavy shoes.

Ian poked his head into the room from around the door of the mudroom. He looked relaxed and younger, with his hair tousled from activity. Her heart did a pitter-patter of awareness. "You ready?"

Allison watched him for a minute too long. He wasn't Lord Hartley at that moment. Just Ian in his element. His gaze turned to one of questioning concern. She blinked and smiled. "I'm done. I'll be right there."

She hugged Mrs. McGregor. "Thank you for a wonderful dinner." She shook hands with Mr. McGregor before she stepped outside.

"Bring her back to see us again soon, son." He slapped Ian on the shoulder as she joined him.

"I hope to do that," Ian replied.

Dark now, Ian dug in his pocket and came out with a flashlight. He directed it in front of them as his hand clasped hers. Warmth flew through her. Ian acted as if it were the most natural thing in the world to hold her hand.

"Come, there's something you might like to see." He directed her toward a small shed. He let go of her hand as he opened the latch. She missed his touch immediately.

"I'll go ahead. Watch your step." He shined the light at the ground as they slipped through the door. He stopped, and she bumped into him. He didn't move away, and neither did she.

A soft noise came from somewhere near their feet. Ian moved the light in that direction. There in a wooden box lay a golden Yorkie mother and her four new pups. "Oh, they're wonderful. How cute. May I pick one up?" She looked at Ian, but couldn't make out his expression in the dim light.

"Sure."

She squatted, and he did as well. Slowly extending her hand, she made sure the mother didn't get upset with her taking one of her babies. The mother watched her closely but made no protest.

"They're adorable. How old are they?"

"A week." Ian ran his index finger over the top of the pup's head and down its spine.

Allison brought the baby up to her cheek, appreciating the warm, soft feel of the downy fur. "I always wanted a dog," she said softly. "But we moved too often to have one. Daddy said it wasn't fair to the dog or us when we couldn't take it with us. When we lived on base other children would have one, but we never did. Turtles, hamsters, and even a small snake for a short time, but never a dog. I've always associated a dog with permanence, a real home."

"I'm sorry." Ian ran the same finger he'd used to gentle the pup along her cheek.

"Dad meant well. I understand now. But it was hard as a kid." Allison placed the pup beside its mother and stood.

Ian straightened as well. "Come, we need to get home. I'm expecting a call."

They started up the lane.

"This isn't the way we came." She mentioned it less out of worry and more from observation.

"No, but you don't want to cross the fields in the dark. Good way to break a leg. This way is a little longer but an easier walk."

Ian held the light, but when she hesitated, he took her hand, pulling her close. "Come here. I don't want you to fall."

Black surrounded them, creating their own little world within the circle of the light from the flashlight. Allison found comfort in the rumble of Ian's voice and the touch of his hand. She found security in knowing he would catch her. For some reason, she wanted these moments to last. The real issue that nagged at her came from the fact she liked Ian too much. He wasn't the man to pin her future on.

"You know you surprised me tonight." She stepped around a small hole.

"How's that?"

"I had no idea you were such a farm boy."

He chuckled. "I'm in my element when I'm working on the land."

"I could tell by your face when you and Mr. McGregor came in." She glanced at him.

"Am I that easy to read?"

"I don't know about that, but I could see it." And she had clearly. "Have you ever thought of selling or delegating Hartley Shipping and living here and working on the land?"

"That dream belonged to a kid. I've reality to deal with now."

"How sad."

They reached the drive of the castle when Allison announced, "I think the first thing I'll do when I get home is adopt a dog."

Ian squeezed her hand. "You should. You deserve one."

For Ian, something about holding Allison's hand felt right, eased him, created a sense of peace. He couldn't remember the last time he'd clasped a woman's hand in a companionable way. Maybe as a child, when he had been with his mother.

Allison walked near enough for him to catch the scent of her shampoo as her hair bobbed. He liked it. Heck, he like everything about her. Even their disagreements. She challenged him, made him think outside his rigid guidelines of life and business. Liked her suggestion he move back to the castle. Impossible, yet it had been thought-provoking. Only someone with her color-outside-the-lines spirit would imagine it doable.

The McGregors had liked her. They'd never warmed up to his ex-wife. And he'd never dared to take another woman to their home.

As he and Allison continued to walk, he wished for more of these easy moments in his life. He noticed that Allison hadn't let go of his hand even when they came close enough to the castle that the outside lamps would allow her to see well enough.

"Let's go this way. Around to the side door. I'm sure Mrs. White will have locked the main one for the night." Ian guided her toward a slate path.

They moved around to the left side of the fortress wall, and he stopped halfway down the side where the stone jutted out in a decorative manner. He reluctantly let go of Allison's fingers before running his hand over a section of the wall.

"What're you doing?"

"You'll see." Seconds later, the concealed passage cracked open.

"Oh man, a hidden passage," Allison said in awe. "I've read about these. But have never seen one."

He chuckled. "This was built for escape during a siege." He lifted the light enough to see her face. "I believe you must've been a handful growing up."

"I was a tomboy."

Ian had never known a woman like Allison. The

women in his circle growing up and as an adult were from families that would never have allowed their daughters to act like a tomboy. Somehow, he'd known this entrance would interest Allison. She wouldn't let being afraid of a spider stop her from an adventure. When had he become so in tune with her that he would register that?

Allison pushed in front of him in her eagerness to enter. Her excitement was almost palpable.

"Would you like to go first?" he asked in mock aggravation.

"Oh, could I?"

He chuckled and handed her the light. "Sure, but please don't leave me behind." He leaned down and said softly, "I'd hate to lose you."

"You better watch it. I might seal you in."

She gave him no opportunity to say anything more before she ducked her head and went inside the dark passage.

"This is sooo cool," reached his ears from the narrow path. He'd come through this way hundreds of times as a kid, so he had no trouble finding his way.

Allison waited for him beside a bookcase in his office. The light reflected her smile. Her eyes burned bright and some of her wild tresses had escaped from their binding. She'd that same expression she'd worn when she'd stared at him from the top of the castle days ago. It excited him and his heart beat faster, awakening that area that had lain dormant for a long time.

"Thanks for showing that to me." She sounded breathless with wonder. "May I go in again? Study it while I'm here?"

Ian grinned. "Yes, but please use this side. I'd rather others not know about it."

She tilted her head. "So why show me?"

"I knew how much you'd like it," he said softly. He stepped closer to her. "You've spiderweb in your hair." Ian removed one and showed her the small white threads on the tips of his fingers. He wiped the web on his trousers.

Placing his hand on her shoulder, he slowly circled his fingers around to her nape. He looked at her for a long moment, searching for acceptance. Her eyes had gone wide, but she didn't retreat. His lips met her partially open ones. She made a small sound before her hands came to his chest. Her fingers gripped his sweater as she pulled him closer. His mouth took hers in a searing kiss.

At her encouragement, Ian ran his hands around her waist. She wrapped her arms around his neck. His tongue searched the seam of her mouth. Allison opened and greeted him. At her moan, he tightened his hold. His shaft rose hard and ready between them. Heaven help him, he wanted her like he'd never wanted before.

He backed against his desk and brought her between his legs. His mouth left hers to travel over her cheek to nip at her ear. She raised her head, allowing him to kiss the tender skin of her neck. The soft purr of her pleasure circled them feeding the fire in him.

Ian pushed at her jacket, wanting to have nothing between them.

His phone rang. That unwanted intrusion brought them to reality.

Allison's hands fell slowly away, as she straightened and move back. "That must be the call you're expecting? You have business to see to. I'll go. Goodnight, Ian."

He let his hands drop to his sides when all he wanted to do was pull her close. Seconds later, he watched Allison disappear out his office door. How far would she have agreed to go if they hadn't been interrupted? One thing glared with certainty, something special had slipped through his hands. He wouldn't let that happen again.

Allison hurried straight to her room, closed the door and leaned against it afraid Ian would follow. If he showed up here, she didn't think she could turn him away. Even now, her heart raced, and she throbbed with need. Just from his kisses.

Sweet, hot ones that promised pleasure—and twisted sheets. What had she been thinking? She worked for him. Their personalities were so opposite from each other. Their worlds were completely different. She didn't need any complications on this project or in her life. Soon she would leave and this thing, whatever it was, would go away. It could go nowhere.

But his kisses! She had melted against him. Begging for more. Her body heated again just remembering Ian's touch. His technique showcased his experience, but at the same time he'd given her his complete attention.

She was doomed.

Drawing a bath, she slipped under the water and grabbed the soap. What would it be like to have Ian's hands running over her? Ugh. Don't think like that. His interest stemmed from him having been at the castle too long without a woman.

Allison dipped under the water. Bobbing up,

she sputtered and pushed her wet hair from her face. No amount of liquid would wash the fantasies of Ian's kisses away. They were too perfect.

By morning she still basked in the warmth of Ian's attention. Her nerves ran ramped at the idea of facing him again. What would he do if she pulled him into a corner and kissed him senseless? She huffed. Not going to happen. No matter how enjoyable it might be. She had bigger things she needed to concern herself with.

She entered the dining room to find Ian sitting at the table eating his breakfast and reading the paper. Her blood hummed through her veins.

"Hello." She turned away, went to the hunt board and picked up a plate. She couldn't see him, but she felt his attention on her. Even her hair quivered.

Before either one of them could say more Roger entered. "I'm glad you're both here." He waved a paper in his hand. "A letter came in the post yesterday. I couldn't find either of you last night. It's from the British Standards Institution."

Allison turned to Roger. Ian's attention already rested on him.

He continued, "They're saying there's an issue with the permits for reconstruction. From what I understand, they need the restoration firm representative and the owner to make an appearance at their office." Concern shone in his eyes as he handed the letter to Ian. "I'm sorry, but it can't be handled locally. I know it's an inconvenience, but ..."

Ian read the letter and passed it to her.

"I can't believe this." She didn't need this right now. The stone was due today.

"Roger, you're sure there's no other way?" Ian asked. "I've a full schedule. I can't move things around with this merger looming. This should have been taken care of."

Roger folded the paper. "I've made calls. I thought it had been dealt with. I'm afraid it's London or nothing."

Ian muttered something under his breath. "It looks like we have no choice."

She understood his frustration. "I've been in constant contact with the local authorities, and he told me we were clear."

Roger spoke to Ian. "Allison and I both scrutinized the documentation when she arrived, and we believed everything was in order."

"Then this means Allison needs to leave with me for London today. I only have tomorrow to deal with this. I won't return for three weeks. I don't want to see the work halted that long."

Allison grasped in disbelief. "What? I can't just leave. The stone's supposed to arrive today. I need to see it. Mr. Welche needs to understand that I'm not backing down."

"Roger can handle that. You can return the day after tomorrow. The stonemasons can examine their options before starting on the wall on Monday. You'll have returned to the castle by then."

Great. This wasn't how she had planned her day to go. Or the next few days.

"I'll take care of everything," Roger said.

"I've had enough trouble with the stone. I really should be here to make sure it's correct. Tuesday would be better for me. Or see if it's okay to show up separately."

Ian shook his head. "I don't want to take any chances. We should go together. Make sure all's correct before I leave the country. I'm sorry, but I only have a small window of time to work with here."

She didn't respond immediately. This had fast turned into an impossible situation. "I need to be here for the stone. Can we leave in the morning?"

"We should leave today, but we can wait until the stone has arrived. Will that suit?"

Allison returned her attention to the plate she had started to fill. "It doesn't seem that I have a choice. I'll see when to expect the delivery."

Ian stood. "Allison, I'm sorry this is inconveniencing you."

"No more than it is you. I'll deal." She put three slices of bacon on her plate and added a piece of toast. "I'm going to eat in my office so I can get a few things done. I'll call as soon as the stone arrives. I'll be ready to go after that."

She started into the hall, but came up short when Ian said, "By the way, we'll be staying at my townhouse."

Allison's heart made a hard thump against her ribs. Stay at his place? After last night! She faced him, "I don't think—"

"No argument. Please. There's plenty of room. It's the same as you staying here." A corner of his mouth lifted as he stepped closer. His next words swirled around them. "If I didn't know better, I might think you don't trust yourself around me."

CHAPTER SIX

Allison admired the confident way Ian whipped in and out among the other fast-moving cars as they approached the outskirts of London. They had been traveling for almost three hours. She didn't mind driving on the left side of the road in the country, but never would she dare drive in central London.

Ian's hand on the gearshift brushed her thigh as he downshifted in tighter traffic. The shock of his touch flashed like lightning through her. A smothering awareness lingered. Ian's knowing look flickered to her, causing a flutter through her midsection. She shifted in her seat, removing her leg from the chances of it happening again. Concentrating on the rhythmic swish of the wiper, she let the sound sooth her rattled nerves.

"I'm glad the stone arrived so we could set off early. Especially with this rain settling in."

"Me too. At least the stone Welche promised showed up. It's still not near enough, but I'll call him next week and push for it again."

"I'm sorry you had to make this trip. I know it couldn't have come at a more inconvenient time."

An apology she hadn't expected. She'd bet Ian didn't often excuse himself in any area of his life. "Things happen. Sometimes you have to be flexible."

"Not something I'm known for."

She grinned. "I'd have to agree with that."

Ian chuckled. "I can count on you to tell me the truth."

"Tell me about this merger." She turned so she could see him clearly.

"I wouldn't think it's your cup of tea."

She chuckled. "You do have a captive audience here."

He shifted out of a roundabout.

"Why don't you try me?"

He gave her a sexy grin.

She flushed, making a mental note that she needed to filter herself for double meanings. "Tell me."

"The merger will make Hartley Shipping larger and stronger. We'll absorb the other company into ours. Every time I do that, it means restructuring. I hate that part. The demands on my time will peak higher than usual for a while. The timing's bad since my sister and kids are coming to the castle. I don't spend enough time with them as it is, and I'll miss out on more."

"Now aren't you glad you told me?"

"Probably more than you enjoyed hearing it." He gave her hand a gentle squeeze. "If you decide to give up engineering, you should consider going into counseling. You're a good listener."

"I don't think I did much, and I don't think that's going to happen."

Warmth ran through her. Apparently, he didn't open up often. Allison was honored he did so with her. Ian did carry a lot on his broad shoulders. By choice or necessity? "I'm glad you told me."

"Family is important. I don't see enough of mine." Allison examined his attractive profile as he spoke. The movement of the muscle in his clean-shaven angular jaw interested her. He had a straight nose above a full mouth. She clasped her hands to prevent herself from reaching out and running her finger along his bottom lip to see if it felt as soft as she remembered. "But I make regular calls home to get all the scoop. We make the most of the time we do have together."

She needed to stop staring at him. Instead she focused on the passing streets that were lined with townhouses sandwiched together and all painted white. They each had a front porch with columns. The only thing that differentiated one place from another was the colors of the doors. Those went from black to red to a navy blue, even yellow.

"Have you spent much time in London?" Ian asked.

"Not as much as I'd like. I've traveled through many times, but I've never had the chance to stay long. The main Hartley Shipping office's here, isn't it?"

"Yes. Along with other offices around the world."

"Do you have to visit those offices often?" He traveled more than she did.

"Often enough."

"Do you mind the travel?"

He waved a hand. "Let's say it's part of the job."

"Soon my idea of travel will be going to the grocery to buy flour to make bread."

"Where did you get this love of baking?" A note of wonder entered his voice.

"My parents wanted us to know our grandparents and cousins, so we spent our summers in the States. My parents grew up in the same small town in Alabama. Gran, my mother's mother, baked almost daily. I spent hours in her farmhouse kitchen. The smell, her company, the whole family thing—I loved it. I missed that time with Gran horribly when I left and looked forward to returning each summer. I baked whenever my mother would let me have the kitchen. Even now, I try to find someone who allows me access to their kitchen wherever I go. Mrs. White's a true gem sharing your kitchen."

"Aw, now I understand. No wonder you're so well-known in the bakery in the village. You worked with Nellie before you moved to the castle." His expression grew thoughtful, like Sherlock Holmes did in the old black and white movies before he solved a case.

"Yeah. Some people go to museums, others to pubs. Me, I find an oven wherever I can."

He chuckled. "That's certainly a dramatic change from engineering."

She nodded. "It is. But for me, baking means roots."

He turned onto a street with a small park within the square then pulled in front of one of those whitewashed houses. The door was royal blue.

"My home." Pride lifted his voice. He slid out of the car and walked around it to open her door.

Standing on the sidewalk, Allison stretched her legs and ran her palms along her simple dress. Next to him, she looked unkempt, frumpy. It wasn't fair for a male to look so good in his clothes. Suave and impeccable — perfect words to describe Ian. Even when he dressed in his hiking wear or an old pair of jeans. If she had a chance, she intended to buy a couple of new outfits. Nothing fancy, just something for a dinner at the castle. Maybe one fun outfit just because.

Ian removed the bags from the boot, refusing to relinquish her suitcase when she offered to take it. She followed him up the steps to the door. A butler opened the blue door and they entered the warmly furnished foyer.

"Welcome home, Lord Hartley," the butler said in a formal tone.

"Hello, Richard. This is Ms. Moore."

The man nodded, and Allison said, "Hi, Richard." She circled the space. "What a nice place, Ian. Not at all what I expected." She studied the modern artwork hanging above antique chests and tables. Interesting. Eclectic. Maybe he wasn't as strait-laced as she once thought. He could see outside the traditional box.

"It's not big and made of stone like the castle," he whispered behind her.

"No. But it suits you. Did you pick out the furnishings?" She ran a finger along a curved edge of a table.

"Yes, but with help."

With a special woman? Leftovers from his ex-wife? Why did that idea cause a sharp prick in her chest? She had no right to be jealous.

"Richard will show you to your room. Please join me for dinner in an hour."

She followed the butler up steep stairs to the second floor. He opened a door midway along the hallway to reveal a medium-sized room that was beautifully appointed with a sleigh bed covered in a modern spread consisting of splashes of brown, green, and orange. Large matching pillows were placed near the headboard.

"If you need anything, ma'am, please let me know." With that, he left her, closing the door.

Allison dropped her overnight duffle bag on the thick rug of mixed colors that complemented the bedding. The bed took most of the space in the room. She sat on the side of the mattress and fell backward, throwing her arm over her eyes. This type of living she could get used to.

A knock at the door woke her. *How could she have gone to sleep?*

The door opened slowly. "Allison?"

Ian. She popped into a sitting position, letting her feet slide to the floor. "Yes." Heat stole up her cheeks. No doubt she appeared as red as the strawberry dress she wore. Pushing her hair back to restore some order, she blinked, bringing things into focus.

"Are you all right?" He stepped into the room. "I got worried when you didn't come downstairs."

"The bed's heaven, and I stayed up late going through papers." She hoped that sounded coherent.

A sly smile covered his lips. "Glad you like it."

She stood. "I'm on my way now."

"Dinner will be served in fifteen minutes." After giving her a long look, he left.

Allison freshened up a bit, arriving downstairs to a small table in the library set for two near the fire. She'd grown used to having dinner with Ian and Roger, had even enjoyed her meal with Ian at the McGregors' but to share such an intimate setting without someone running interference…

Ian's charm alone could prove dangerous, have her doing and saying things she shouldn't. Last night had been a shining example. Swallowing hard, Allison stepped to the entrance of the room.

The glow of the fire highlighted Ian's sculpted features, reminding her of an invincible knight of old. She stood speechless. He was so…male. She needed to stifle the urge to go to him and crush her lips to his. Had he thought of their kiss as often as she had during the day?

At the castle, she'd caught him watching her work from the ground. Another time, while on the scaffolding, she'd noticed him on the roof surveying the workmen haul stone. Even from that distance, it was like a high voltage line hung between them, causing a jolt to her system. That time he'd lifted a hand, and she'd returned his wave. She'd wanted to climb down to talk to him, but thankfully, one of the workers called, preventing her. She couldn't have Ian thinking she was chasing him.

Now she stood observing him like some voyeur peeking through a window. She'd fought living at the castle, but she'd delighted in unlocking its secrets. And some of Ian's. Like a puzzle she enjoyed fitting the pieces together. She'd liked the picture she'd put together and learned that her first impressions of him had been wrong.

Her heart fluttered. She'd grown to respect him. He loved his family, was a good friend, a solid businessman, and when he wasn't consumed by having his way, he'd a sense of humor. The only thing she'd like to see, for his sake, was for him to take time to enjoy life more.

The desire to touch him had her clasping her hands. She couldn't give in to that need. It would lead to places she couldn't stay. She'd no stopping sense regarding him.

Ian spotted her and stood. "Allison, how long have you been standing there?" He gave her a rakish grin that made her remember their kiss. She liked that particular twist to his mouth. "If you continue to move around so quietly, I'm going to request that you wear those ugly boots all the time."

She blushed but walked toward him. "I've been here half a second, so don't let your ego get carried away."

He chuckled. "Where you're concerned that could never happen." His voice had gone deeper, and his accent more pronounced. "You've a way of keeping it in check."

"I apologize if I've damaged it."

He grinned and stood with his back to the fire. "I wish I could believe you mean that."

Not since being a teenager had she wanted something more feminine to wear. Her simple clothes had always been adequate but now... Now she wished she looked more presentable...put together...sexy?

"Come on over by the fire. You seem chilled," Ian said. "This old house can be cool even on a warm day. I had Mrs. White send my housekeeper here the recipe for your iced tea." He lifted a pitcher. "Would you care for a glass?"

How thoughtful of him, to think of that detail in his busy day. An attack of nerves made her hands shake as she walked toward him. "Yes. Thank you."

Their gazes met and held. That undeniable current flowed between them, so strong it bunched her stomach, released the wave sending tingles out to the tips of her breasts, fingers, and toes. The urge to run pulsed strong, but the desire to step closer to Ian proved greater.

Ian's eyes held warmth, appreciation, and maybe anticipation. Her middle did a flip as she stepped next to him. She could grow to love being near him.

"I elected for us to eat here. I hated for the staff to go to so much trouble setting the dining room."

"Very nice, I mean considerate of you."

He grinned. "I try when I can."

How true. Now she knew him better, and she found Ian thoughtful. Not at all as self-centered as she had once thought.

Moving to stand behind one of the chairs at the table, he pulled it out for her.

With shaky knees, Allison sat. Ian's hand lightly brushed her shoulder and he moved away. That innocent touch heated her enough to make her blood hum. Her response to him had to stop, or she combust.

He took the other chair. "I hope you found everything you need in your room."

"It's very nice. Thank you." She lowered her head and narrowed her eyes. "Ian, is the room I'm staying in... your bedroom?"

"Yes. How did you know? I told Richard to clear my things out."

"The bathroom items gave it away. I can't stay in your bedroom."

"Of course, you can. I'm down the hall, so you don't have anything to worry about."

"Why would you give me your room?" What was he up to?

"It's the only one with a connecting bath, and I thought you might like it more than having to go across the hall."

Once again, he'd surprised her with his kindness. "Thanks for thinking of me, but I'd rather you change rooms with me."

"I'm hungry. Let's stop arguing about something that won't happen and eat."

"But—"

A middle-aged woman carrying a tray chose that moment to enter. She placed it on a serving stand near them.

Ian rose and hugged her. "Hello, Edna."

She offered him a broad smile.

"May I introduce Allison Moore. Allison, this is Edna, the best cook in all of London."

Edna patted Ian's middle. "Aw, go on with you."

Ian gave her another quick hug. "I'll handle the serving and leave the tray in the kitchen. You head home to your family. I'm sorry for showing up on such short notice for dinner."

"No problem."

"I'll say goodnight then." She smiled at Allison and nodded to Ian. And quietly closed the door behind her as she went out.

Ian stepped to the tray. "Let's see what we have here. Salad, chicken, and vegetables with a raspberry tart to finish."

"Sounds wonderful." Allison scooted her chair out.

"Keep your seat." He smiled. "I'll serve."

Allison settled in place. Ian sat their salads to the left. It looked wonderful with greens, pecans, blue cheese crumbs, and sliced strawberries. He then placed their main plates in front. The chicken leg and thigh were browned to perfection with herbs scattered over it. Sweet potato cubes filled out the plate with braised yellow and zucchini squash slices. It all looked divine.

She inhaled. "It smells wonderful."

"Edna thinks I'm going on with her, but she's an outstanding cook." He took his seat, picked up his fork, and they began to eat.

"Oh my, this is good." Allison took a bite of the potatoes.

Ian raised his eyes. "I'll let Edna know you enjoyed it."

A few minutes went by before Allison spoke to Ian. "Where're you off to for this big merger meeting?"

He met her gaze. "Hong Kong. Ever been there?"

"No. That's one of the few places I've missed."

"Would you like to go sometime?"

"Yes, very much. I may talk about not traveling, but that doesn't mean I don't enjoy vacations."

"You don't think you're going to get bored in

your house baking bread all the time?" He forked some chicken into his mouth.

Allison shifted. "I want to try. How about you? What do you want?"

He gave it some thought. "I like to travel. When I do, I'd like to have more time to enjoy the places I go. I want my mother and sister to be happy. I want this merger to go well."

"Admirable. Especially wanting your mother and sister's happiness. It's good you have a place with shared memories like the castle. My grandparents' house is the closest my family comes to having something like that. My parents only bought their first house five years ago, so it doesn't hold many memories. The hazards of the military. I think you have something pretty special."

His gaze met hers. "How like you to speak your mind."

Her head shifted to one side. "I'm sorry. Sometimes I say things when I should keep them to myself."

"No. I like to hear what you have to say. It's always thought-provoking."

She continued to hold his gaze. "Even when it's not what you want to hear?"

Ian nodded. "Especially then. When you have a title, people don't often speak freely to you. That's what I like best about you. I don't have to wonder where you stand on a subject."

Her brows rose. "And that's a good thing?"

"Yes, it is. Refreshing, in fact." He took a sip of his drink. "I could get used to having you around."

"You'd get tired of me pretty quickly."

"I doubt that." Ian tone implied he meant it.

She looked around the beautifully appointed room. "I don't think I would fit into your life. We only know each other because your castle needed repairing. As Lord Hartley, you travel in a different space than I do. Look at this meal." She waved a hand over the table. "Prepared by a cook when I do my own cooking."

"I'd eat soup and sandwiches every meal if I didn't have someone to cook for me."

She chuckled. "And I would if I did. I couldn't afford anything else if I did. Plus, I like my boots. Which I know you don't."

"I do prefer seeing your green tipped toes." He grinned over his glass. "I could probably get used to your boots."

She returned his grin. "I doubt you felt that way a couple of weeks ago."

"Maybe not. Let's say that you were a bit of a surprise. Your boots and hard hat too."

"Is that your way of apologizing?" She took another bite of chicken.

He watched her a moment. "I wouldn't say that."

She put her fork down and picked up her wine glass. "I figured you wouldn't."

He smiled. "You're starting to know me so well. Are you ready for dessert?"

"If you are." The familiarity between them had increased. She'd been trying not to become more involved with Ian; instead they were growing closer.

Ian took her empty plate and replaced it with another holding a tart. He exchanged his plate as well, then joined her again.

Allison cut into the tart, forking a piece into her

mouth. "Mmm, beyond wonderful."

"It is."

Her attention went to him, and she found Ian watching her with a heated gleam in his eye.

Allison flashed hot under his gaze. She suspected he referred to something different. Over the next ten minutes, they finished their food with little conversation. She finished the last bite with a sigh.

Ian studied her with a grin on his face. "Would you like me to see if Edna would share the recipe?"

Allison brightened. "Would you? Please."

Ian's smile grew. "Glad to."

"Thank you. What time do you want to leave in the morning?"

"At eight. That should give us time to get to the office before it opens. We'll have the morning traffic to contend with."

"Meet you in the foyer. If you'll point me in the direction of the kitchen, I'll take care of our dishes."

"No, Richard will see to them."

"Then, I'll say goodnight." She stood. "Please tell Edna the meal was delicious."

"I will." Ian came to his feet. "I'll walk you up."

"That's not necessary." Could she resist Ian if he asked to come into her room? His room?

He moved to stand beside her. "Still I'll do so."

She proceeded Ian up the stairs, the entire time conscious of him a step behind her. Every fiber in her hummed with awareness. Her body had become so in tune to his nearness. Relieved to reach her door—correction, Ian's door—she quickly opened it. "Uh, thanks for dinner. See you in the morning.

Goodnight."

He leaned toward her.

Ian wanted to kiss her. She couldn't let that happen, even if she wished him to. If she did, she'd never let him stop. Everything about him was addictive for her. A relationship with Ian could only become messy and end badly. She turned her head. "Ian, we shouldn't do this."

His eyelids lowered. "I'm not sure I agree."

She had to resist him, or she might lose her heart. Not a part of her life plan. Settle down, get a dog, see if she could find a nice man around her new home. No rush to the altar. Even if she gave that up, she'd never fit into Ian's world. "I'm only here for a little while."

"We could make that time more enjoyable."

"I've too much on my plate, and you do too. You're getting ready to leave the country."

"Maybe so, but this is the time we're allotted. I'd prefer not to waste it." He took one of her hands, his thumb trailing over the top of it. "You and I both know there's something between us. Last night in my office confirmed it."

Allison couldn't disagree. Still, if her heart became involved, she'd be devastated when she had to leave. And leave, she would. She'd worked toward settling in America for too long. A plan she had no intention of giving up. Their paths in life veered in different directions.

She gave him a wry smile. "To what end? I want a home and family and you need a Lady Hartley that I'd never measure up to, even if we could make more of this. That leaves us with a one-night stand." Allison shook her head. "I'm not good with easy sex."

Ian lifted her chin with the tip of a finger until she had no choice but to look at him. A fire of desire burned in his eyes. He wanted her. The idea was empowering. She shivered. "You're overthinking this. If you change your mind, you know where I am. I won't change my mind."

He brought her into his arms. His kiss ran deep with persuasion as he tugged at her bottom lip before he let her go seconds later. Allison's body buzzed with pleasure and throbbed with need. And begged for more.

"Think about it, Allison." Ian's words brushed against her ear before he turned and walked down the hall.

Allison leaned against the doorframe as she watched him leave. Her body screamed to call him back. Yet her heart relied on her good sense not to have it broken. Entering her room, Allison closed the door with a soft click. Had she just refused the best thing that might have ever happened to her?

Ian's night had been long and sleepless. He'd hoped Allison would come to him. To his disappointment, she had not. The need for her throbbed in him whenever she came near and desire pulsed when she wasn't. He had wanted women before but never with this driving need.

Allison tested him, made him step out of his comfort zone, and even pushed him to meet her wit. She added excitement to his rather dull, always focused on business life. Besides her sex appeal, which she certainly had in abundance, she made him feel alive. When he was with her, he forgot all his responsibilities for a while. Something he rarely had the pleasure of doing.

When she met him for breakfast in the dining room that morning, he found satisfaction in the fact that she didn't look any better rested than he. Had she lain awake longing for him?

Without much discussion, they had their meal and left for the British Standards Institution office. Already open when they arrived, and in less than an hour, they were leaving with their business complete. They'd gone to a great deal of effort for two signatures. Yet both had been required.

"I must hurry to my office for a meeting but I'd like to take you out to dinner." He cupped her elbow as they went down the steps.

"You don't have to entertain me. I'll be fine on my own. I might head back to Hartshire early."

Ian couldn't let her do that. He wanted to spend time with her, especially with him leaving for three weeks. "The train doesn't run until later this evening. Don't go yet. Please let me take you to dinner tonight."

"That sounds nice, but I thought if I stayed, I'd try to see a play. I don't get to do that often enough."

Ian didn't like the idea of her pushing him away. "I should finish with my business in time for dinner and a show. Do you mind having company?"

She took too long to answer for his well-being, but she finally said, "That sounds nice."

He would have hated to admit out loud how her answer relieved his mind. "Great. Can I drop you somewhere now? At the house?"

"I'll accept a ride to Piccadilly Square."

"That I can do."

They returned to his car.

Twenty minutes later, he pulled to the curb, and she climbed out. Before she closed the door, he said, "I'll call you this afternoon. You can tell me where to meet you for the show." He reached into his pocket and pulled out some pound notes, handing them to her.

"I don't need that."

Ian wasn't surprised by her rejection. "Please take it. I'd like you to buy something nice as a thank you for making the trip into London."

"That's not necessary."

He glanced into the rearview mirror. "Allison, I can't stay here arguing with you without getting a ticket. Take it and use it on yourself. The show tickets."

She looked around, then snatched the money. "You aggravate me."

Ian laughed. "No more than you do me. Enjoy your day. See you in a little bit. Wear something amazing."

Allison huffed and slammed the door.

When had he last enjoyed sparing with a woman this much? Never. Seeing Allison again couldn't happen soon enough. He drove away with a grin on his face, eager for evening to come.

CHAPTER SEVEN

The buildings of the City of London were casting evening shadows when Ian's cab driver pulled to the curb in front of the Strand Theatre. He'd decided not to drive so he wouldn't waste time finding parking. Allison had called and left a message to meet her there at seven-thirty. He hated that he missed the call. For the first time, his mind wasn't on his work. Most of the day he'd spent thinking about what she might be doing.

He'd no idea what to expect from the evening, but he looked forward to spending time with her. Normally surprises ruffled his feathers, but with Allison he found himself eager to embrace changes. A new concept for him, in his planned world.

He had started toward the box office when he spotted her. How he'd not noticed Allison earlier, he couldn't imagine. As always, she stood out in a crowd in more ways than one.

She wore an orange-red dress. Straight vintage twenties with a three-inch fringe around the bottom. To make her stand out further, she had a lime green lacy shawl with red rosettes wrapped around her shoulders. She never failed to astonish him.

Her russet hair fell around her face in a riot of curls. He itched to touch a strand—even more he wanted to run his fingers through its silky length. A good thing she kept it confined most of the time because otherwise, he might have made a fool of himself touching her constantly.

Allison walked toward him with a smile on her face. Her outfit highlighted her gorgeous curves. Her breasts filled out the V-neck of her dress without revealing too much but hinting at more creaminess.

"Ian?" Her husky tone made his manhood tighten.

"Uh...Allison, you look sensational." He generally wasn't speechless, but this time...

"Thank you." She made a slight curtsy. "You don't look half bad yourself."

He'd taken the time to change into the extra suit he kept at his office.

"Come on. The show's about to start." Allison had already turned toward the theater.

Ian placed his hand on her waist. "Right. What're we seeing?" He hadn't thought to check the marquee. Allison in her sexy dress had blinded him to anything else but her.

"*Stomp.*"

"Pardon?"

"You know, the show where they beat garbage can tops together?"

Ian raised his brows and worked hard not to

groan. Not his idea of a show. Musical, mystery, drama, not garbage cans.

Allison continued to chatter happily. "Haven't you heard of it? It's one of the longest-running shows in New York. I've never had a chance to see it."

Ian couldn't help but get caught up in her enthusiasm. Somehow, she made garbage cans sound like a great idea. Soon they found their seats. Allison had purchased the tickets and chosen ones up front and center. Even if he wanted to escape, he wouldn't have a chance.

At the first round of dazing noise, Allison leaned forward as if she wanted to join the people on stage. "This is so cool." Awe filled her voice.

As the show continued, Ian found that he enjoyed the inventive way the musicians managed to make music from everyday items. But despite all the activity on stage, Allison held his attention more.

When her hand brushed his leg as she shifted to see what happened on his side of the stage, he captured and held it. She gave him a shy smile and didn't pull away. Her smiled seduced him in the same way he wanted to seduce her. The difference in the size of their hands reminded him of Allison's tiny stature. Yet the force of her personality made her a giant.

With the final bang of metal against metal, Allison hopped to her feet and clapped almost as loud as the drums.

He couldn't help but grin. When he joined her, she grabbed his arm with both of hers, pulling him to her in her enthusiasm. Her breasts pressed against his upper arm. Scalding heat shot through him, centering below his waist. Allison mesmerized him with her bright eyes and wide smile. He wanted her.

"You think I'm nuts, don't you?"

"If you are, I'm right with you." His lips softly touched hers. The kiss should've been a quick peck, but with the feel of her supple lips below his, he lingered, taking their kiss deeper.

Allison leaned further into him, tightening her grip on his arm, escalating his desire. His mouth settled more firmly over hers. He gripped a handful of her dress, pulling her to him. She met his lips with a gentle push of hers.

Breaking the kiss, Allison stared into his eyes. Wonder, anticipation, and possibilities all resided there. Ian started after another meeting when she placed a hand on his chest.

"Ian, I think someone's trying to get your attention."

He glanced over his shoulder. Seconds later, he resisted the urge to take her by the hand and run for the door. He'd no doubt he'd hate everything about what would happen next.

Allison shifted away from Ian. Just as well. They shouldn't had been kissing so passionately, especially in public. But she'd wanted Ian's kiss so badly. Fighting their attraction no longer appealed to her. Ian made her feel desirable, more than enough. Heady stuff to have a man like Ian want her. His kisses left her with no doubt that he did.

She watched as a tall, leggy brunette with perfect hair and the slick lines of a panther sauntered down the aisle toward them. In a throaty voice, she asked, "Ian Hartley, is that you?"

"Risa." Ian offered the woman a polite smile that didn't quite reach his eyes. Their special moment vanished.

"I thought so, but I couldn't imagine you coming to a show like this." The woman studied Allison as if trying to figure out why Ian came with her.

"Not my usual fare, but I enjoyed it." Ian turned to Allison. "Especially the finale."

Allison gave him a shy smile. He left her no doubt that he meant their kiss, not the show. She'd enjoyed the finale as well.

"It was great, wasn't it?" Risa continued to look at her, but her nose had moved slightly higher.

Ian's hand settled on Allison's waist as if providing moral support.

A portly man joined them.

"Hello, Arthur. How've you been?" Ian stepped forward to shake hands.

Allison had the sense that Ian liked Arthur far better than Risa.

"Great. It's good to see you. It has been a while." He smiled at Allison. A genuine one.

Ian moved nearer, standing close enough she could feel his body heat. "Risa, Arthur, this is Allison Moore."

"Nice to meet you," Arthur offered with a smile still on his face.

Allison liked the man right away.

"How about we go over to the Ritz for a late supper? That would give us a chance to catch up." Risa smiled sweetly as she placed a hand on Ian's arm.

Ian shifted so that Risa's hand slid away. "Allison, would you mind?"

What would she be getting herself into? But Ian seemed to want to go. "Fine. I'd love to see the Ritz."

"Never been to the Ritz? I can't imagine. It's my home away from home." Risa's gave her a kind but insincere smile.

Allison recognized a catty woman when she saw one. This woman was the breathing definition of the word.

The Ritz Hotel embodied everything Allison had ever heard and everything that she wasn't. From the twinkling lights outside to the marble floors inside, and the elegance of the furnishings signifying class and restraint. Not her element, but Ian looked right at home.

His hand rested warm and reassuring at her waist as she walked beside him. Their group followed the hostess to a small dining room close to a window that overlooked Green Park. Lights lit the trees, giving it an otherworldly look. Ian held out her chair at the white, cloth-covered table.

Allison soon learned Ian and Arthur had gone to Eton together. Listening to the stories of their youth she found interesting and entertaining. Even as Ian and his friends talked, he made a point to find some way he could include her in the conversation. A few times, he took her hand and squeezed it reminding her he hadn't forgotten her.

After dessert, Allison excused herself to go to the restroom, and Risa joined her.

"Would you wait for me?" Risa asked, while in the powder room area.

Allison agreed, reluctantly. She could only

imagine what the woman had in mind.

While returning to the dining room, Risa stopped Allison with a touch to her arm. "So," Risa leaned toward Allison, and her voice lowered to a conspiratorial tone, "have you known Ian long?"

"Not really."

Risa gave her an expectant look as if waiting for Allison to say more. When she didn't, Risa continued, "How did you meet Ian?"

"I'm the constructional engineer redoing his castle."

Risa studied her a moment. "Ah, I wondered. I was Judith's best friend."

"Judith?"

"His ex-wife. He didn't tell you about her?"

Allison had zero interest in revealing personal details. She started to walk away, but the woman grabbed her arm. "You're not his usual type."

"We're not involved that way." But was that true? The more she stayed around Ian, the greater his sexual pull.

"Not yet. I've known Ian a long time. He's not the kind of man who lets a pretty woman escape. And you're a pretty woman. You're different enough that he considers you entertaining, but he'll marry someone with the right bloodline. That will be someone like me. I plan to be there when he's ready."

Allison turned cold and studied at her a moment. "I wish you luck with that."

Ian glanced at Allison, who sat quietly beside him during the taxi ride home. Her hands rested in her lap. A vault door had closed and locked between them when she returned to the table after going to the restroom with Risa. He'd asked her questions trying to make conversation, but she murmured polite replies in return.

What had that devil said to upset Allison? One minute she had been laughing and smiling at his antics, and the next she'd closed him off. She seemed to enjoy herself right up until she went off with Risa. Arthur had pulled him aside before he and Risa left them to say, "This one's special."

Ian couldn't agree with him more. His involvement with Allison made him a little nervous. Still, he didn't like this distance between them. Especially after they had started opening up to each other.

The taxi let them out in front of his townhome. Allison rushed headlong through the front door before he could pay the driver. He hurried up the steps, catching her by the elbow before she started up the stairs. "Hey, would you like a glass of iced tea before going to bed?"

"I don't think so. I'm tired, and we both have to get up early." She wouldn't face him. "I need to sleep."

"We don't have to be up *that* early." Ian kept his voice low and steady. The last thing he wanted was to fight with her, but he didn't want to give her up yet. They wouldn't see each other for weeks. "I'll drive you to the train station."

"I can call a taxi."

Ian sighed heavily. "Allison, what happened? What did Risa say?"

"Nothing important."

"I knew better than to let you be alone with her, but I couldn't stop her going to the restroom.

She and my ex were best friends for a while. If not for Arthur, I wouldn't have agreed to dinner. She encouraged Judith to run around on me. Told Judith I wouldn't divorce her because I'm a Hartley. When I did, Risa came after me thinking, I'd marry her. Which I won't."

Allison shook her head sadly. "You don't need to tell me this."

"But I want you to know." He peered into her eyes. She must understand.

"She said I wasn't good enough for you. That you're playing with me. I know that. Maybe not the playing part but we don't make sense for the long run."

"Don't believe anything she has to say. She has nothing to do with us."

"She still thinks you'll marry her someday. I don't know her background but I'm sure she must have the pedigree that you need for another Lady Hartley."

"Hell will freeze over before that happens," he spat.

"Ian, I don't want to get involved with any of this. I have a job to do, and then I'm going home."

He moved closer. "Are you finding excuses to run from your feelings for me?" He studied her for a moment. "Or could it be you're running from yourself?"

His hand went to the upper part of her arm, then slid to her elbow. There, his thumb swirled at the crease. She trembled but didn't move away. Nudging her toward him, he stepped closer, closing the gap between them. Allison's eyes had turned dark green like the spring pastures after a rain. His fingertips barely touched her flesh as he brushed his hand over the softness of her skin on his way to her shoulders.

"Ian, I don't think—"

His lips found hers. Her mouth parted, and he took advantage of the opportunity to deepen the kiss. She sank against him, her arms circling his neck. Her fingers fed through the hair at his nape as she pulled him closer and took control of the kiss.

Allison's tongue danced and played with his like they had been partners forever. He grew rock hard and he pressed against her. His hand went to her waist and pulled her snug, leaving her no doubt of what she did to him. She let out a soft sound of pure contentment and pleasure.

Male satisfaction shot through him. She wanted him.

Seconds later, Allison rested her hands on the plane of his chest. Her push, the lightest of touches. His hands that had dipped low on her hips, stilled. His mouth left hers with such reluctance he tugged at her lower lip. Ian groaned his disappointment. It took all his resolve as a gentleman not to scoop her into his arms and carry her up the stairs. But this must be a decision they both made.

"Let's go upstairs." The words whispered against her lips.

Allison stepped back, putting distance between them, and his hands fell to his sides. Disappointment grew in him.

"Ian, I'm sorry if I led you on. This isn't a good idea. You're my client. I need to focus on the job you've hired me to do. I don't think us doing this—" She waved a hand between them. "—is smart. Tonight, just reinforced how unrealistic it would be."

He propped his arm over the square top of the newel post, acting far more casual than he felt. Placing a foot on the first tread, he tried to allow her the distance she said she wanted. "That may be so, but you aren't any less affected by our kisses than I am. There's something between us, and I'd like to explore it."

Allison blinked. He watched as resolve entered her eyes once more. "To what end? One night of hot sex?"

His gave her a sardonic smile. "We might have more, if you were willing to find out."

"More? Come on, Ian. You know better than that. We're from two different worlds. I'm sorry. I can't pretend differently."

Ian watched with regret as Allison's sexy bottom swayed as she climbed the stairs. He gripped the newel post until his knuckles ached. Could she be right? Much too complicated.

He needed peace. Allison would never bring that to his life. She was too vivacious. He needed a woman who'd give him an heir, represent the Hartley name, and handle social events. Risa might be right that Allison didn't fit that role. But he'd never choose Risa. Reluctantly, he realized that his world could quench Allison's spirit. The restrictive atmosphere and expectations would stifle her.

Still, that logical thinking didn't dampen the burning need in him to have her, feel her against him. He'd take what he could get if she'd offer it.

Later Ian sat before the cold fireplace in his study. He'd come there instead of following Allison up. Otherwise, he might have done something he'd regret. Something like go to his room, let himself in, and slide into *his* bed next to her.

He clenched his jaw. Right now, she scented his sheets with lavender. Would the scent linger till his return?

Entering her bedroom, or really Ian's, Allison closed the door, leaning against it. She'd longed to turn and race down the stairs back to his arms. She'd wanted to take his hand and pull him up the steps, to the lovely bed in front of her.

But she couldn't. Dan had destroyed her self-esteem, and even though Ian had started to repair it tonight, she'd let some woman she didn't know with an agenda knock her down again. Why?

She'd more strength than that. To have Ian at all... How wonderful? To see if the spark he lit in her flared, just once. Would that be so bad? Wouldn't this be the time? Wouldn't she always wonder?

The larger question, could she go to bed with Ian and walk away? No strings attached? She could if she wouldn't let her heart become involved. Maybe she needed to get him out of her system. One and done. Enjoy the experience and move on. Just like her restoration projects.

Summoning her courage, she left the bedroom. She made no noise as she moved. Downstairs? His temporary room? She waited, stalling. Maybe common sense would return. What Ian offered might be more than she could handle.

She turned to re-enter her room when Ian stepped to the top of the stairs. Even from here, his male magnetism pulled at her. His head turned slightly to one side in question as his look bore into her.

"Did you want me?" His voice held a note of

hopefulness.

Heavens, yes. "I, uh…"

Ian strode long and quick to her side. He stood close, but didn't touch her. "Yes?"

"I thought…" Why didn't the darn man take her in his arms? Get her out of this awkward moment.

"Yes?" His breath brushed her temple.

He'd make her say it. Put the words out into the world. "That I want…"

"Yes?" The single word sounded strangled.

"To take you up on your offer."

Ian cocked a brow. Her lips thinned. The temptation to kick him in the shin built. He was enjoying her discomfort. "Which one?"

She looked at his chest. "For one night. You and me."

Seconds later Ian gathered her in his arms. His lips found hers in a hot and deep, all-consuming kiss that left no question he still wanted her. His arms wrapped around her waist as he lifted her tightly against him. They came up for air long enough for him to take her hand, give a gentle squeeze and lead her to her door. Ian kicked the door closed. "Now that wasn't so hard to say, was it?"

Spinning her, Ian backed her against the door, molding his body against hers. His gaze locked on hers. The wildness in his eyes registered in her center, causing a deep flutter that went straight to her core. She scanned his face. As cool and controlled as the lord always tried to appear, the tight rein he held on himself showed in the tension of his jaw and the brightness of his eyes. He wanted her.

That only heightened her desire. She shifted against him, prompting a tremor in him that she felt as well. *She* did that to him. Her heart ramped up with the heady thought.

"I've missed too much sleep thinking about having you." His lips met hers in a soft but demanding kiss.

Allison ran her hands over his chest, across his shoulders and up the sides of his neck. Her fingertips rested against his pulse, beating like a tribal drum before moving to cup his cheeks.

Ian unleashed a rough low predatory sound. His hands dipped on her hips, lifting her into him. The thrill of his hard length between them empowered her.

She pulled his face to hers, meeting his mouth. She parted his lips and entered. He tried to take control, but she resisted. Removing her lips from his, she ran her mouth along the curve of his face to his ear. She whispered, "You taste good."

"Not as good as I know you will as I kiss every part of you." He stepped toward the bed, bringing her with him. Her lips returned to his. As if his eagerness got the better of him, he lifted her, carried her, and pinned her to the mattress. Never releasing her lips.

Allison giggled. She felt Ian's smile against her mouth before he pulled away. Rolling to the side, his hands remained at her waist. His lips dipped to hers again as if he couldn't get enough of her. She liked that idea. He gathered the dress around her waist. As the material climbed higher, the coolness of the air made her shiver when it touched her heated skin.

Ian smiled at her. "You're beautiful."

That he thought so heated her blood.

He stood and pulled her to a seated position on the high bed.

"What..."

Stepping forward, he moved between her legs. Her fingers gripped his biceps, as she watched the emotions play across his face. Desire was evident, along with a tenderness that circled her heart.

Her hands traveled along Ian's muscled arms to play in the hair above the collar of his shirt. With one finger, she followed the edge of his collar, touching skin and ending at the V of his shirt. She opened the top button. His breath hitched.

She continued the process of touching, stopping, releasing, and moving downward as her gaze held his. With his shirt open, she looked her fill at the large expanse of chest with a light dusting of hair. Need vibrated through her, pooling at her center.

As if they had a mind of their own, her fingers touched the warm skin covering the bands of muscle. Fanning her hands, she traveled across his torso, lightly brushing over the hair at his sternum. She loved the way his body flexed at her touch. She leaned into him and inhaled deeply.

Ian's hold at her waist tightened.

Allison smiled. She blew out slowly, letting her breath flow over his skin.

"You're killing me." Ian's words whooshed harsh with emotion.

Her smile grew with satisfaction. She placed a whisper of a kiss on his chest. "Hush, I'm enjoying myself." Her fingers moved to his pants, unbuttoning and pushing both them and his underwear down.

Ian stepped out of them. All glorious male, his manhood stood tall and thick before her. She wrapped her hand around his length.

"Enough," he hissed as he pulled her to her feet. Gathering her dress, he whipped it over her head and let it drop the floor. Just as quickly he removed her bra. He paused a moment to admire her, his fingertips brushing along the bottom curve of a breast. Seconds later he wrapped his fingers in her panties, and in one swift motion added them to the pile of clothing.

Jerking the drawer of the bedside table open, he pulled out a package and covered himself. Laying her on the bed once more, his mouth covered hers, and he entered her, "Next...time...slow."

Allison panted as he slid inside her. Her eyelids dropped. She matched his rhythm. Climbing, grasping, she topped the peak and floated downwards as if a leaf on a breeze. She'd found heaven.

Ian's body stilled but remained in her.

Allison opened her eyes to find Ian braced on his hands, looking at her with an almost silly grin on his aristocratic mouth like a man well pleased with himself, and confident he'd satisfied a woman.

She smiled. "That—"

"You made it clear." He placed a quick kiss on her lips.

Lifting her hips, she pulled away, appreciating his length. "Well, Lord Hartley, it's your turn."

Ian didn't allow her to maintain control. He thrust into her hard. Allison wrapped her legs high on his hips, taking him deeper. He felt so wonderful. That groaning, curling need built again. At Ian's powerful shudder, she joined him. His body slumped to cover hers, the weight of him felt so right. Finally, Ian rolled to his side, and shifted further onto the bed, gathering her close.

"Stay with me," he whispered, before giving her earlobe a nip with his teeth as he fondled her breast.

Allison snuggled into him, smiling. Just like Ian to make it a decree instead of a question. "You're in *my* bed."

He nuzzled her neck. "Mmm, I am, and I like it here."

Ian woke to a pleasant warmth wrapped around him. Allison's head rested on his shoulder, and one of her bare legs looped around his. He could see her toes—now painted orange. He grinned. Last night he'd sucked on those sweet little digits, making Allison giggle. Even now, he stirred at the memory. Ian twisted his mouth. He'd stayed with her all night. The first time he'd done that since his marriage. He couldn't bring himself to leave Allison.

During the early hours of the morning, he'd woken her, and they had shared their bodies once again. Allison was all he'd ever dreamed of in a lover. Warm, attentive, and giving. He'd reached heights he'd never gone to before. Sadly, she'd only offered one night.

Allison shifted beside him. He rubbed his chin over the glossy, silkiness of her hair, one of his favorite things about her. "Good morning. Did you sleep well?"

"Mmm. Well, but not much." Her thigh rubbed his leg as she moved to look at him.

Ian chuckled low in his throat. His chest swelled with the pride of a man supremely satisfied—and who'd given satisfaction. Because of Allison, he felt that way. He played with a corkscrew strand of her hair as her head rested on his chest.

"Tell me something."

She made a noise of agreement.

"Why don't you have a husband or someone important in your life?"

She rose, pulling the sheet over her breasts. "You want to know that? Now?"

"I don't understand how someone as intelligent, beautiful, and extraordinary in bed could be single. Have the men you have dated been idiots?"

Allison's shoulders shifted. She let the sheet slip, giving him an enticing peek at one of her breasts. "Extraordinary? I like the sound of that."

"It's true. So why has no man claimed you?"

"The last one questioned my femininity. He didn't like my pants, hardhat, or the fact I worked outside. Basically, I wasn't woman enough for him."

"Bloody hell, that's laughable." He pulled her to him. "I've never known a woman more feminine or sexy. He wasn't enough of a man for you."

Ian hated that she'd carried the idea she inadequate for so long. There couldn't be anything further from the truth. He then went about showing her how perfect he found her.

Sometime later, they lay in bed catching their breaths.

Ian ran a finger over her stomach. "As much as I hate it, we need to get out of bed to get you to the train station on time."

"I'll get a shower and meet you downstairs." Allison quickly scooted away from him. Something in her voice made him think she had started pulling away from him, not just physically but mentally.

"Mind if I join you?"

Her gaze jerked to his as she squeaked, "Share?"

Had she never shared a shower with a man? The idea that he would be her first appealed. Ian climbed out of bed and offered her his hand. "Come on. I'll let you get in first."

Allison hesitated a moment before she took his hand, but not before she picked up his shirt and held it in front of her. As they entered the bath, she said, "I should invite you. After all, it's my shower."

Allison never disappointed him. He shrugged. "Technically, it's *my* shower."

"Giving me your room made it very convenient for you." She stood behind him, but he heard the teasing in her voice.

"Convenient?"

"To finding your way into bed with me."

Ian faced her. "You came looking for me, remember?"

Her mouth formed an O like a fish, and she had the good grace to blush. Ian found it rather cute. He tapped the end of her nose. "Now, in the shower with you."

Allison still clutched the shirt.

He tugged it, dropping it to the tiles. "This needs to stay out here."

She stepped into the shower, and he followed. Picking up the soap, he began to wash her. Allison leaned against him as he soaped her breasts. Sweet time went by as the water cooled.

"As much as I'd like to stay right here forever," he brushed the tip of her breast with his lips, "we need to leave in forty-five minutes. That should give us enough time to dress and have breakfast."

She turned and kissed him over his heart.

Ian's lips found hers. They could dress quickly and skip breakfast.

CHAPTER EIGHT

Allison had returned to the castle three days earlier in time for her weekly meeting with Mallory and Jordon. Would they see what she hadn't told them yet? Were her feelings for Ian written all over her face? He'd only been gone a little while and she already missed him.

Jordon, the most perceptive of her two friends, caught on first. "You went to bed with him? I hear it in your voice."

"Oh, Al." Mallory's tone turned much softer. "You haven't fallen for him, have you?"

"More than I should. We agreed to one night. I'll get over him."

"Famous last words," Jordon said.

"He's left for Hong Kong for three weeks. By then the tower should almost be done. I'll handle it."

Mallory's face grew larger in the picture. "So how—"

"Mallory!" Jordon cried.

Allison couldn't help but smile. A warmth washed over her. "Perfect."

Jordon groaned, and Mallory giggled.

"You're in love." Sympathy rose in Mallory's voice.

Allison shook her head. "I won't allow it. It'll never work. It's only an attraction."

"He'd be crazy not to want you," Mallory said.

"I've never seen you glow. You *are* glowing." Jordon looked at her with wonder on her face. Jordon continued, "Careful. I don't want to see you hurt."

"What would I do without you guys?" She was blessed to have such supportive friends.

"Keep us posted," Mallory said. "I've got to go."

"Me too." Jordon waved, then both faces disappeared.

Allison stared at the blank screen. What would Ian want when he returned? Maybe he wouldn't come to the castle. Let Roger handle things. She hadn't heard anything from him. She probably wouldn't. One night had been their agreement. No matter how much she wanted more.

The days crawled by and turned into two weeks. Still no word from Ian. She survived by keeping her focus on the job. The nights when she had time to remember were more difficult.

Allison hadn't seen Ian in sixteen days, eight hours, and ten minutes when she sat in the kitchen of the castle having a glass of tea and waiting out an afternoon storm with Mrs. White. The sound of feet running through the dining room caught her attention. She looked at Mrs. White, who smiled and started toward the door. Thankfully she hadn't made it yet, because a boy of about seven and a girl a little younger burst through.

The towhead boy pulled up short and the girl right beside him. "We're here."

"Why, hello, Jonathan and Margaret." Mrs. White leaned over and opened her arms. The children smiled and stepped into her hugs. "I wasn't expecting you until next week. You have surprised me."

The youngsters laughed.

"Mum wanted to come."

The girl with blond ringlets turned to Allison. Jonathan followed her gaze. He asked, "Who are you?"

"I'm Allison. And who's this with you? Your sister?"

The boy made a big gesture of nodding his head.

"It's nice to meet you both."

The door opened, and a woman walked in who favored Ian enough that Allison had no doubt it was his sister. She could only be described as a classic beauty. The Hartleys had good genes.

"Miss Clarissa. Welcome home." Mrs. White enveloped her into her ample body.

Clarissa returned the hug then stood back. "It feels good to be here. I know we're a little early, but I was ready for the kids to have some space to run."

She looked at Allison. "You must be Allison. I'm Ian's sister Clarissa. I've heard all about the woman who's doing amazing things with the castle. My brother doesn't gush about many people."

He'd talked to his sister, but Allison hadn't

heard from him. Even Roger hadn't said much about talking to Ian. Was the man in a hole? Allison thought he'd at least check in about her work on the castle.

Allison couldn't help but blush. "Hello." Just what had Ian said about her? Had he confided in his sister about their night together? No. She stood and extended her hand. "I can't imagine Ian gushing about anything."

Clarissa took her hand. "This will be the last time we're so formal. I feel like I know you already. You do know my brother. Gushing might be an exaggeration, but he has told me what a good job you're doing on the tower."

"Another couple of weeks and the damaged area of the castle should be ready for use."

Mrs. White pulled a large metal tin off a shelf and spoke to the children, "Come on lovelies, how about we have a little tea party to tide you over until dinner?"

"That sounds nice," Clarissa said. "We don't want to put you to a lot of extra trouble. Let's have it in the kitchen."

Mrs. White set out the plates and cups.

Clarissa took a bite out of her cookie and looked at Mrs. White. "These are wonderful. I don't remember you making these before."

The older woman gave Clarissa a big toothy grin. "That's because I didn't bake them. Allison did. She's a sensational baker. It's one of her recipes."

"Maybe you could share some of them with me. I enjoy trying new ones, but I'm not very good at baking. Mrs. White used to push me out of the kitchen when I couldn't get it right."

Mrs. White blushed. "Now, hen, you know that's not true. But I'll say that Allison's baking makes me look like a poor cook. She even had Ian making bread."

Clarissa's mouth dropped open, and she stared at Allison in disbelief. "He did what?"

Mrs. White chuckled softly.

"I must head to work. Clarissa, Jonathan, and Margaret—it's a pleasure to meet you." Allison quickly escaped. She had no interest in explaining hers and Ian's relationship even if she understood it, which she did not.

That evening their meal in the dining room Allison would remember as one of the liveliest she had since childhood. She dreamed of one day having the same type in her own home. It had been years since she'd experienced this contentment.

She could hardly stop smiling. Ian's niece and nephew asked questions constantly and moved the tableware around and poked at each other. Their energy seemed endless. Clarissa took most of their antics in stride, only using a forceful voice when they went too far.

Only the lack of Ian's presence put a damper on the evening. Would he be as happy sitting at the table as she?

Allison hadn't spent much time around small children. She didn't get to see her nieces and nephews often. A heartache filled her at all she had missed. A few days here and there hadn't been enough. She'd make a point of hosting them when she had a house.

"Uncle Ian's coming home tomorrow. He said he'd take me to see the lambs," Jonathan announced.

Heat washed over Allison. Her heart rate jumped a notch. *Ian...home.*

"He said we'd visit to Mr. Mc..."

She almost picked up Jonathan and hugged him in her excitement. "Mr. McGregor's farm?"

"Yeah."

"That sounds like fun." *Ian... home early.*

"You want to go?" Jonathan gave her an expectant look.

"I'll have to see what your Uncle Ian says."

Ian would be here tomorrow!

Allison anticipated Ian's return all day. Her middle fluttered like swallows taking flight every time a car came up the drive. Could it be him? She ached to see him when she knew she shouldn't. They'd made no promises. They'd had their night of passion. He hadn't called her. Yet she wanted more.

She settled into her special place on the rampart wall with her back against the tower and studied the darkening sky that for once didn't hold clouds. Maybe Jonathan misunderstood about Ian's return. She pushed those thoughts away. Ian had become the center of her thoughts without almost any effort on his part and against her better judgment.

The voice she heard in her dreams came from the direction of the stairs. "May I join you?"

Ian. Despite her body jumping into overdrive, Allison managed to act calm. How had she missed his return? That didn't matter now. He was here. She shrugged a shoulder. Did her wariness show? "As I said weeks ago, it's your castle."

He chuckled. "So it is. But somehow, I think

you have more say."

He came within touching distance, yet he didn't reach out. She had to remind her body to behave. Everything in her wanted to wrap her arms around him. "How was your trip? You're home sooner than expected."

"Yes." He appeared perplexed by that idea. "I needed to come home." He studied her with such intensity that it made her shake. Did she disappoint him?

He'd once told her she was perfect. She'd believed him when his body showed her.

Taking one of her curls between two fingers, he let it slip through them.

She sucked in a breath. "Did you know Clarissa and the kids came early?"

Ian stepped closer. "I spoke to her yesterday. Is that really what you want to discuss?"

Allison didn't want to talk about anything. She wanted him to kiss her. Take her to his room and make love to her all night. But she couldn't say that. Wouldn't say it. She hated to admit to herself—and to Ian—that she'd desperately missed him.

More than once, she'd thought she'd heard his voice in the hall or hoped a call coming in would be him. She looked at the stone floor, suddenly shy. "I don't know. I was trying to catch you up on things around here."

"I'd rather catch up on things I've missed." Ian took one of her hands and tugged until she stood.

Heat shot through her. Every nerve ending aware of his skin against hers.

Not letting go of her, Ian sat in her vacated space and nudged her back until she sat between his legs. He wrapped his arms around her, bringing her against his chest while clasping his hands in front of her waist. "Comfortable?"

His breath warmed her ear. She had no idea what he thought, but she adored his arms wrapped around her. Her greatest fear averted, that he'd treat her as if she didn't matter anymore, she leaned into him. "This is a mighty big castle for us to need to sit in the same spot."

The rumble of his chuckle vibrated against her spine.

"All I want is to touch you again." His voice came out as a low caress over her skin.

Her heart thumped harder. He still wanted her. Had she said one night? Ian had just agreed to it. What did she want now? This. Moments like this for as long as they'd last.

Seconds went by before he murmured against her ear, "I've missed you."

His words tugged at her womb. No more than she had him.

Neither of them said anything for a moment. "The polite thing would be to say you missed me too."

"Is that so?" She put a teasing note in her voice.

"Indeed."

"I'm afraid, Lord Hartley, that your ego might grow larger."

"Ms. Moore, around you, it isn't my ego you should fear growing."

She giggled.

"Tell me what you know about the heavens." He nuzzled her neck just below her ear.

Only that I'm there when I'm with you. "Not much. I like to come up here to think."

"And what were you thinking about this evening?" His finger trailed over the ridges of her knuckles, dipping into the hollows and out again. "Me, maybe?"

Allison scoffed. "I see your ego *is* still in good form."

"You keep it in check."

"I was thinking that maybe your phone's broken."

"How's that?" He sounded perplexed by that idea.

"You didn't even call to ask about how the reconstruction was going." *Or check on me.*

"I couldn't. If I spoke to you, I would've left in the middle of the merger. Instead, I rushed through with lightning speed to get back home. It was difficult enough to get through what I did without speaking to you."

Allison's body heated. He'd missed her too.

He ran little kisses along her neck, the last one ending in a nip on the tender skin beneath her ear. She shivered. Without thinking, she tilted her head so he'd have better access.

"Allison..." the whispered word pleaded, "turn around."

Her body tensed in anticipation. She twisted to face him but remained between his legs.

Ian's hand went to the elastic band holding her hair away from her face. Pulling it free, he flung it over the side of the wall.

"Hey, I need—"

"Shh. I'll buy you another." His fingers slid into her hair and cupped her head. He ran them through her curls until her hair tumbled around her shoulders. Against her lips, he said, "I like it down. All wild and free like you. Allison, kiss me. I've missed you so."

She sealed her mouth to his. Slanting to the side, she deepened the kiss. Ian's fingers tightened at her waist. Her hands moved along his bare forearms, enjoying the feel of him. Letting her fingers travel further, she reached his biceps and tucked her fingers under his knit sleeve.

Ian tugged at her shirt, pulling it from her pants. The sun had set, leaving the last glow of the day. The cool air touched her skin, making her shiver—or was it Ian's touch? One of his hands caressed her spine, heating her.

He took control of their kiss, his tongue taking possession and sending her body into that dream world only Ian could create. Heaven help her, she'd been lost without him. She rode blissfully in the headiness of his kiss.

His hand left the small of her back and journeyed upward, leaving a swath of hypersensitive skin behind. Touching the edge of her bra, a finger worked its way under and stopped.

Ian's mouth left hers to travel along the line of her scoop-necked shirt, leaving kisses over the top of her breasts.

Allison arched and groaned. Her hands held his head as her body reached, begged for his attention.

His fingertips beneath her bra scanned the edge until he reached the front closure and flicked it open. Finding her mouth again, his tongue danced with hers. He broke away long enough to strip her shirt and bra over her head.

Allison quaked from the knowledge that Ian studied her. She reached for her shirt.

Ian caught each of her wrists in a gentle clasp. "Don't. You're beautiful, especially against the backdrop of the fields. Like a wood nymph coming to life at dark."Ian waxed poetic, and she loved it. Everything about his words made her feel desirable, *enough*.

His head dipped forward, and his heated mouth surrounded her hard nipple. He gently sucked. Her middle tightened. Her head dropped back, and she released a sound of pure animal pleasure. She felt Ian's smile against her skin.

He let go of her hands and cupped the globes of her breasts in his hands. "Loveliest things I've ever seen. Soft, creamy, and pure perfection."

IIis mouth found her skin again, his tongue rolling around her nipple, making her breasts ache. With a gentle tug, he released her, then moved to the other one, giving it equal attention. His mouth returned to hers, giving the same caress to her bottom lip that he had to her breasts.

Ian certainly knew how to say hello after a long absence. Allison ran her hands over the wide, hard plane of his chest. Finding a button, she pushed it until it released. Without enough room to touch him, she pulled at his shirt until he lifted his arms so she could remove it. Her hands immediately roamed his torso, enjoying the feel of him. She sighed, then placed a kiss over his heart.

He chuckled. "Find something you like?"

"Uh-hum." He must have appreciated her response because his manhood jumped against her stomach.

"Bloody he..." He pulled her so tight, they could have been one. His mouth covered her face in kisses and came to rest on hers again.

Dazed by Ian's lovemaking, she wasn't sure she'd heard it at first, but now she registered the sound of a car approaching. "Ian..."

His lips left hers and moved to her earlobe. "Mmm..."

"Clarissa and the kids are coming up the drive. We have to stop."

"Why?" He ran his hand along the bottom edge of her breast.

Allison almost forgot what she had been saying. "Ian," she took his head in her palms, holding it so he had to face her. "Your sister is here. You need to talk to her. The kids are eager to see you."

He said some words low enough that she couldn't make them out, but with such force they could've burned her ears. Disappointed swamped her as well. Moving back, she made room for him to stand. He picked up her clothes and handed them to her. As she untangled her bra from her shirt, he pulled on his clothing.

Allison fumbled with her bra. Ian stopped her before she closed the front clasp, pulled her to him, and kissed the side of her breast. His fingers looked even larger as they worked to close the latch.

"Have experience at this, have you?" Allison asked over the top of his head.

"Some, but never a time more memorable or important than this one."

Ian had a way of saying the right thing. Her

glow from that statement could light the eastern coast of America if it could be harnessed.

He helped her on with her shirt. Allison giggled.

"What?" he took her hand.

"The great Lord Hartley almost got caught making out on the roof of his castle."

He took her hand. "And he would've continued to do so if he hadn't been interrupted."

The frustration in his voice thrilled her. They hurried to her bedroom door before the front door closed.

She gave him a gentle push. "You need to go. I know they want to see you."

"You're not coming?"

"No, I've some work to do, and you need this time together without the hired help around."

"Hired help?" His voice turned sharp. "You've some of the strangest ideas. That title no longer applies."

"Thanks for saying that. I didn't really like you bossing me around all the time anyway."

"Oh, I'm still the boss." He gave her a quick kiss and a wink. When she started to speak, he tapped her on the nose. "Don't ever forget that."

"I just let you think you are."

"I won't argue that point." He sandwiched her between the door and the hard plain of his body, standing close enough to make it clear his arousal hadn't diminished. The ardor of his kiss bruised her lips. "You know this isn't finished, don't you?" he whispered in her ear, before leaving her to stand in an Ian-induced daze.

During the evening dinner and afterward as the family sat in the living room, Ian was hyperaware of Allison watching him with a dreamy expression on her face. What was she thinking? This expression wasn't the one she wore when they were in bed together. More like the one she wore when she enjoyed a wonderful piece of pastry. The type that tightened his chest and made him ask himself "what if".

Allison puzzled him. She ordered the men about with authority, yet she wore a hot pink hardhat. She handled blueprints and files, then looked equally at home in the kitchen. Even now, she blended in with his family. As if she belonged. He didn't want her to do that. If she didn't, it would make it far easier when she left.

He couldn't believe a man had ever told her that she wasn't feminine enough. Sex appeal wafted off her. Allison drew him toward her on sight. If Ian ever saw the man who'd spurned her, he would set him straight and remind him that Allison belonged to him. *Belonged*? Did she really? They'd never talked of the future. Could they have a future?

His weeks away had been endless. He'd never left a business meeting unfinished, but he couldn't stand the distance away from Allison any longer. He'd feared she might return to America before he could see her again. So he'd left his lawyers to finish the details.

When he arrived at the castle, he'd headed to the top, knowing she'd finish her day there. At first, he hadn't known if she would welcome him. He feared she would want to stick to their agreement. As far as he was concerned, that wasn't going to happen. His body had ached for her every night. A grown man shouldn't need a woman so much.

Jonathan and Margaret sat in his lap, and he worked to control his reaction to Allison as he told them all the things they could do while at Hartley Castle.

"Soon, get to wade in the river." He tapped Margaret's nose. "But only if an adult is with you. You can visit the sheep at Mr. McGregor's and build a fort in the woods."

"I don't have any friends to help me," Jonathan whined.

"Margaret can help you." Ian had forgotten how nice his childhood had been when the family had come to the castle. One he would be glad to share with his niece and nephew. He should have been doing that before now. When had his world become so filled with business and responsibilities that he couldn't see anything more in life?

He glanced at Allison. His gut tightened. That wistful look remained on her face as she watched them. It heated and disturbed him at the same time, making him have thoughts of the future. He had no intention to offer her one. Allison had her plans laid out, but if he decided he wanted her to stay would she consider it? Could she be the wife he needed? Would she want to produce a Hartley heir?

Would Allison even consider fitting into his world? Would he want her to? He liked Allison just as she was. Asking her to conform to his often times restrictive sphere wouldn't be fair. Did he want her enough to try? He hadn't thought about what *he* wanted in so long he didn't know where to begin.

Looking away stopped him from going to Allison, flipping her over his shoulder, and carrying her up the stairs. She'd cased a spell over him.

Clarissa stood. "Children, it's time for bed. Tell Uncle Ian, Uncle Roger, and Ms. Moore goodnight."

Allison smiled at the children. "You can call me Allison. That's friendlier than Ms. Moore."

"Okay, let's go." Clarissa took their hands.

"Uncle Ian, will you tuck me in tonight?" Margaret asked.

"Do as your mother says, and I'll be up in a few minutes." He wanted to tuck Allison in. Would she welcome him to her bed? He *would* be asking.

Soon after Clarissa and the children left, Allison excused herself with a nod to Roger and him. Ian watched her leave. He turned to see Roger watching him.

"Allison is a special person," Roger offered.

"She is. She's doing a great job on the tower."

Roger cleared his throat. "That's not what I'm talking about."

Was Roger interested in Allison? Despite their long friendship, a knot of jealousy formed in Ian's gut. He struggled to keep his voice even. "Are you interested in her?"

A slow grin formed on Roger's mouth. "No, but I believe you are. You haven't taken your eyes off her all night."

"We're just good friends."

"Then you might want to make that clear to her. She deserves better than to have her heart broken." Roger gave him a stern look, something Ian had never received from him.

"I don't plan to do that."

Roger sat forward, his elbows on his knees. "Maybe not, but I suspect she leads with her heart.

She may not realize what's required to be a Hartley."

Roger's words left a bitter taste in Ian's mouth. "Allison can take care of herself."

"That may be so, but she seemed pretty infatuated with you tonight."

Ian couldn't argue with that. A fact he liked. "I'll take care of Allison. She's *not* yours to worry about."

Roger chuckled, stood, and headed toward the door. "But she *is* yours."

Ian watched the flames in the fireplace. There had been plenty of women after Judith but none had touched him as Allison did. What he believed would only be a casual fling had turned into something greater. Not one of the women in his past had made him think of the future until Allison came along. He was in deep. What should he do?

Later that evening, Ian slipped into Allison's room. This was his castle, and he had to sneak around. The idea irritated him. He wasn't ashamed of his desire for Allison, but it wasn't something he wanted to share yet. He hadn't liked what Roger had implied. Was he using her? Did she want something more than he couldn't give? All they had talked about was one night. Now he would be asking for more.

When he opened the door, he found Allison sitting in the center of the bed reading papers. She wore the pajamas she'd wore that morning he'd gone to her room at the hotel. Her glorious hair fell around her shoulders. He hardened instantly.

A saucy grin covered her lips. "Ian, I didn't hear you knock. What're you doing here? I'm not in your room again, am I?"

"No, but you should be," he growled as he closed the door behind him. "You deserve the best in the castle."

"I thought we agreed to one night."

He stopped beside the bed. "I'm used to all my agreements being in triplet and notarized. Otherwise, they're null and void. Anyway, I'm here on tuck-in duty. First Margaret, now it's your turn." His gaze lingered on her. "Scoot over, and I'll pull down the covers."

She placed the papers on the bedside table and did as he requested.

"Now, climb under."

Allison moved over to lay on the sheets. She left him a tantalizing view of her cleavage in the V of her shirt. He braced his hands on either side of her head and leaned in for a kiss. He would leave after a kiss if she wanted it that way, but it would kill him.

"Agreements are so overrated." She wrapped her arms around his neck, pulling him to her as she gave him a deep wet kiss that seemed to go on forever, yet not long enough.

CHAPTER NINE

Ian had only made an overnight trip to London, yet it seemed to last an eternity. The entire time all he could think about had been hurrying back to Allison.

He'd asked her to go with him, but she'd declined feeling she needed to oversee all the final details of the restoration. He had been disappointed, but he understood. She took her work seriously. Right now, he didn't want anything more than Allison and a bed.

When he hadn't spotted her pink hat bobbing at the top of the castle or not found her in her office, he headed for the kitchen. He pushed open the swinging door, his heart beating faster. Allison stood behind the work counter, adorable with her hair pulled back and flour floating around her. The powder hanging in the air made him think of magical fairy dust. Somehow his world righted again. Allison had unquestionably put an enchantment on him.

He couldn't fathom how much he had missed her.

Coming to Hartley Castle held bittersweet memories for him. Sweet because there'd been many good times with his brother and father, bitter because they were no longer there. Then along came Allison.

She looked right in his kitchen, his home, his castle. With him.

Mrs. White stood beside the stove stirring a pot. "I've enjoyed sharing my kitchen. I'm sorry you're not staying longer."

"I've enjoyed spending time with you too. Feels like I'm in my grandmother's kitchen again. The only problem is I can't seem to control the amount of bread I make." Golden brown loaves were lined up beside her.

"I'll have to take them to the Saturday market if you keep up this pace," Mrs. White said.

Allison glanced up. Her gaze met his. A soft smile formed on her lips.

Peace filled him. He had returned to where he belonged.

Her look didn't waver as she brushed her hair off her brow, leaving a streak of white. Pink crept into her cheeks. He couldn't get enough of her. Had she missed him too? He'd even had his associates repeat themselves during a multimillion-pound meeting all because Allison took up so much space in his brain. "Hi."

"Hey." The word crossed her lips like a wisp.

The desire to kiss her senseless almost overcame him. He glanced at Mrs. White.

"Welcome home," the older woman smiled.

"Hello, Mrs. White." He straightened and walked into the room and faced Allison across the counter. He had to place something between them, or he'd act on his need. "I can see that my renovation engineer still can't stay on the job when I'm away."

Allison's eyes twinkled as she reached for the apron around her waist and began to wipe her hands. "Lord Hartley." The note in her voice made it clear she wasn't using the title out of respect. "I can assure you that the repairs haven't stopped in your absence. We've received all our stone shipments, and everything is on schedule. Want to see the progress?"

He grinned. A chance to have her to himself. "Ms. Moore, I have no doubt they've gone well under your guidance. Give me a minute to change, and you can give me a tour. And you might..." he picked up the soft dishcloth laying on the counter and walked around to her, "want to check a mirror before you talk to the men." He put a finger under her chin and turned her face so he could gently run the cloth across her forehead. "You've flour everywhere."

Her cheeks turned an adorable pink. "Thank you."

His voice dipped lower. "I like when you blush for me."

Pulling the cloth from his hand, she used it to swat his forearm.

He laughed and leaned his hip against the counter. "Did you use your flour cutter thing on this dough?"

Allison smiled. "Not this time. We made yeast dough today. I'll use it when Mrs. White shows me how to make a mince pie tomorrow."

"That sounds good." He glanced at the older woman. "Mrs. White. I'm famished. What's in the pot? It smells wonderful."

"Chicken and rice soup. Allison shared a family recipe."

"Really?" His gaze returned to Allison. "I had no idea you had so many talents. Are you hiding more?"

She gave him the saucy smile he was so fond of. "Every woman has to have some surprises."

Mrs. White chuckled softly.

He glanced beyond Allison to his housekeeper. "Mrs. White, why don't you make an early evening of it? Allison and I can have a bowl of soup and some of this wonderful smelling bread after we review the repairs." *And other things.*

He needed time alone with Allison, and he wasn't ashamed to admit it. Afterward, he would catch up with Clarissa and the kids. The castle had become too small in the past week for the privacy he wished for where Allison was concerned.

Allison's eyes narrowed. Was she wondering what he was up to? He gave her a predatory leer. Her eyes widened as the touch of pink on her cheeks deepened. She licked her lips, and he hardened.

"What about Clarissa and the kids?" Mrs. White asked.

"I spoke to her earlier, and they're eating at a friend's. Roger's away on business. So, Mrs. White, you're free and clear."

"Thank you, sir. I'd planned to visit my sister this evening. She'll be glad to have me earlier instead of later."

Ian straightened, giving Allison a pointed look. "I'll meet you in the hallway upstairs in ten minutes?"

She nodded slowly.

Would she resist him? Had she decided to stop their affair while he was gone? He wanted a few minutes with her. No, he wanted more. "Excellent."

A few minutes later he stood outside her bedroom door. "Allison?"

"Almost ready."

He heard her scuffling around. "May I come in?"

"I'm putting on my boots. Just a sec."

"You don't need your boots." He'd just have to take them off again.

"Why not? I'll need them on the roof." The door swung open, and the air whooshed out of him as if she'd sucker-punched him. Allison had taken the time to loosen her hair so it flowed around her shoulders. A touch of makeup highlighted her eyes and a hint of pink gloss covered her smiling lips. Warmth filled his chest.

He took her by the shoulders and backed her into the room, closing the door. "I have other things I want to examine before I check the castle's progress."

She widened her eyes. "Like what?"

"Your body." He kept moving her toward the bed.

"Weren't you questioning my performance during your absence? I want to show you what I can do. It'll be dark soon," she cooed.

Ian chuckled. Heaven help him, he'd missed her. He brushed a kiss across her temple. "I'd love to have you show me what you can do. All of it."

He continued moving until they reached the edge of the bed. Then he took them down together, making a small bounce. Allison circled his neck with her arms. "I dare you to question my abilities again, Lord Hartley."

Allison encouraged him to roll so that she lay on top of him. Her hair hung around his face. She gave him that look of delight she'd used when she discovered her find at the village market. His heart tumbled. He made a fist in her hair and tugged her to him.

"I would guess that this isn't how a proper Lady Hartley would act?"

"I'd want her to."

She nipped at his bottom lip. "So, tell me Lord Hartley, exactly what do you require in your Lady?"

"Are you applying for the job?"

"I'd need to know the requirements first to say." She gave him a quick kiss to the lips.

"Hmmm." His brows came together drawing lines in his forehead. "She'd need to appreciate the history of the Hartley name. Need to understand the value of upholding the name. Need to care about me, be true to me, and want my children. A partner."

"That's a pretty generic and short list for such an important job. What about breeding? Or a wonderful hostess at a dinner party? Wearing the right clothes, doing philanthropic work? Oh, and where does that incidental part like...love come in?"

"You've given this a lot of thought." Was

Allison hoping she might stay with him? Did he wish that?

"Not as much as you would think. Most of it I have known all along."

"If the job were offered would you consider taking it?" He watched her carefully.

She looked at his chin instead of into his eyes. "I don't know. I'm not sure I'm qualified. It's far different from anything I've ever done."

"I think you'd make an excellent lady, if you wanted." His hand ran along her side. "One thing, I have no interest in having my wife act like a lady in my bed."

"You don't need to worry about that with me." Allison grinned before her mouth found his.

She tasted so good. Her hands traveled over him. He returned her kisses with equal need. She offered her mouth, giving him full access to the sweetness while accepting and returning the same pleasure. Her hips pressed against his sex. Soon he stripped her, drove inside her and surrendered to the power and the light that could only be Allison.

Much later after checking on the repair, they went to the kitchen for their meal. Ian watched Allison across the table as she bit into a slice of bread. He knew no one else like her. Quirky, she saw everyday things in a different light, and she certainly didn't dress like anyone else. He wouldn't change a thing about her. She added spice to his life.

"Despite my earlier reservations about choosing your company, you've done an outstanding job. If I've not apologized earlier, please accept my heartfelt apology now."

"Wow, what a formal statement, Lord Hartley."

She smiled at his wince. "But it held a ring of sincerity so I shall accept it."

"Thank you for your graciousness." He bowed his head with a smile on his face. Business had never so fun. In fact, with Allison around his happiness quotient increased. His chest tightened. He shouldn't be thinking like that.

"My pleasure."

They both laughed.

He sat back. "I wanted to ask you something."

"No, you have to do your own dishes."

Ian smiled. "Let me make it clear as the lord of the castle I don't do dishes. It isn't that anyway. I've a business associate who has a manor house near the Dover coast. He's having trouble with some foundation work that must meet the new regulations. He isn't sure he's getting the correct information from the contractors he's spoken to. I'm asking this as a favor to me. I wondered if you'd would talk to him? It's a chance to give your company more work. I've told him what a good job you're doing for me."

"I see."

"One more thing. We're meeting at a business dinner next week. Would you go with me?"

Allison pretended to give it a great deal of thought. "I don't know—"

"Here I thought you liked me. I've not worked this hard for a girl to go out with me since I was a teen."

"Maybe that's the problem." She cupped his face. "Girls have flocked all over you, and you think you can have any one at any time."

Ian leaned into her personal space but didn't

touch her. Holding her gaze, he dropped his voice low. "I don't want just anyone. I want you."

She sighed. "Ian, in all seriousness, I'll be glad to review your associate's plans, but I don't belong at one of your business dinners. I don't run in your social circle. I wouldn't want to embarrass you."

"Sweetheart, you couldn't embarrass me. You're a breath of fresh air in my stale life. I'll proudly have you on my arm." To his amazement, he truly meant that.

"I don't know."

"Just think about it, okay?" Where did she get the idea that she might shame him? Her ex-boyfriend really had gotten into her head. Or was it all his talk of the importance of being a Hartley?

"I will."

They returned to eating.

Ian sensed Allison watching him. "What?"

"Hmm. With the right persuasion." She licked her bottom lip. "I might say yes to your invitation."

He grinned. Standing, he took her hand and pulled her to her feet. "Have you ever made love under the stars on top of a castle?"

The next Tuesday night, Ian waited in the great hall for Allison to join him. He hadn't seen enough of her in the past couple of days. He'd been busy, and she and Clarissa had spent a great deal of time cloistered away in Clarissa's room. They'd become fast friends. The only time he'd had alone with Allison had been at night in bed.

Now, he paced the great hall waiting on her like a young man on his first date. He wanted the evening to go well. Especially since she'd revealed her nervousness about fitting in. Allison suited his everyday life fine, and with this dinner, she would have entered the business part of his world as well.

At a noise on the stairs, Ian turned. Clarissa.

Her short laugh carried in the steep-ceilinged room. "You should see your face. You look so disappointed. You've got it bad." She studied him closely. "And my guess is you're fighting it - hard."

Ian wrinkled his brow. "I don't know what you're talking about."

Clarissa chuckled. "You do, but you refuse to admit it." A serious note entered her voice. "Ian, you do realize that every woman isn't like Judith. Remember how happy Mother and Father were. Don't waste your chance for happiness. You deserve some. And that's your little sister lecture for today." She stood on her toes and kissed him on the cheek. "Oh, by the way, Allison's not far behind me."

Clarissa was right. He shouldn't let his poor relationships affect the present, but letting go of the negative could be difficult for him. He had responsibilities to the family and his future. And Allison's work took her around the world. Her new home base would keep them even further apart. She'd worked so hard for those dreams; how did he stand a chance?

At the clip of heels, his attention returned to the top of the stairs. Allison descended looking gorgeous. The emerald satin dress she wore had pleats up the front, making the material hug her slim body. Over it she had a matching jacket of the same color. Her outfit couldn't have been more faultless for a business dinner. She outshone any of the models he'd ever dated.

He let out a breath, relieved she hadn't worn

one of her practical dresses or even the eccentric orange-red number from London. He'd wondered if she might not be clad conservatively enough for the group tonight but hadn't wanted to insult her.

For some reason, he found he missed the surprise of her usual dress. He'd hate to think she restrained herself on his behalf. Her hair flowed around her shoulders held from her face by a bright multicolored African patterned scarf. The shoes she wore had a similar design. Ian grinned. He'd never wanted a woman more.

She nervously pushed at her hair. "I'm sorry I'm late. I had trouble with my hair." She huffed. "It's not used to being dolled up this much."

Ian stepped forward to meet her. "Allison, you look amazing."

Her smile warmed him from the inside out.

"And you," she ran her fingers on the edge of the lapel of his black suit jacket, "don't look half bad yourself."

Ian kissed her on the cheek. He glanced at Clarissa, who grinned like a doting mom. He offered his arm and escorted Allison to the door. To Clarissa he said, "Don't wait up."

Allison had decided she'd make the most of the evening. Even if Risa might be there. Ian was *her* date. This meeting meant something to him, and she wanted to help him. Making him proud was her focus tonight. Showing him, she could fit in among his peers.

She wanted him to feel her support. Somehow, she'd gotten the idea he hadn't always felt that way. That he carried the weight of his world on his shoulders alone.

The restoration had gone well. She'd leave soon, and she intended to make the most of the time she had left with Ian. She cared too much for him, but she would worry about that later. Tonight, she meant to soak up all of him she could to have as many memories as possible.

At the car, she made a point of touching his hand where it rested on the door handle. "I'm looking forward to meeting your friends."

His eyes narrowed. "Is something going on here I don't know about?"

Allison gave him what she hoped looked like a coy smile. She'd never used one in her life on purpose and had no idea if she had achieved it. "No, I'm trying to be a good date."

As he pulled onto the main road, she ran her hand over the fabric covering his thigh. "This material must be expensive. It feels wonderful." The large muscle in his leg jumped beneath her palm.

His hand captured hers and held it on his leg. His fingers lay between hers. This time he slowed the car. "Now, you *are* making me nervous. Did Clarissa encourage you to do something?"

When she tried to remove her hand, he held it in place and moved his fingertips slowly along the length of hers. Maybe she'd gone too far. "No. I just wanted to let you know that I like that you trust me enough to take me to your dinner party."

"Of course, I trust you. You're the most brilliant woman I know."

Allison glowed under his praise.

He leaned over and kissed her. "The sexiest too."

Heat, red hot, settled between her legs. If she wasn't careful, she might embarrass them both.

He returned to driving. "You know, I think we should check into an inn for the night."

Allison smiled. "Mmm, that sounds nice." She pulled her hand from his and brushed the pulse point along his neck.

"You keep that up, and we won't make the dinner. Until I get you alone, that's all I'll think about." He captured her hand again. "We're both going to need some self-control."

"You know, Ian," her voice dropped to an old movie starlet level, "sometimes you have more control by giving it away."

Ian couldn't believe how Allison tied him in knots. With her amazing hair flowing around her shoulders, making him itch to touch it, to her sexy green dress and the small touches she gave him when she thought no one watched. He had the hots for his date. All he could think about taking her to the nearest inn to show her how he felt.

Allison made the perfect dinner partner. He'd introduced her while cocktails were served and she'd put each person she met at ease. Her sincerity and genuine caring showed when she spoke. Then there was that enticing accent that made the sound of her voice even sweeter. She blended in well in his world. As if she belonged there.

As they entered the private dining room of the hotel, Ian placed his hand at Allison's waist. She smiled and walked regally beside him. For the last ten minutes, she'd engaged in an animated discussion with Preston Westworth, one of Ian's most difficult work associates. She'd charmed

Westworth during drinks to the point he wanted to sit next to her during dinner. Her actions weren't about seduction or wanting the attention on her, as his ex-wife had been. Instead, Allison used her wit and intelligence to win the man over.

Currently, she faced the pompous Westworth and talked with her hands to make a point. Ian might've worried she would say something that could damage his relationship. But Westworth had a smile on his face, and his belly jiggled as he let out a bark of laughter that stopped conversation along the table. When was the last time Ian had seen the old coot smile, much less laugh?

Ian wanted the man's business. Westworth had used another shipping line for years. For almost as long, Ian had tried to convince Westworth to change to Hartley Shipping. Allison just might make that happen for him.

She glanced around and smiled at him before she went back to listening to Westworth as if he told the most profound story. Ian might have been jealous, except every once in a while, her hand slipped under the table to run along his leg. His manhood reacted. Allison hadn't forgotten about him.

By dessert, it became difficult for Ian to follow his conversation with Lucinda Upchurch, the widow of one of his father's oldest business relationships and the hostess sitting on the other side of him.

"I'm sorry, Lucinda, did you say something?"

She laughed. "About three times, but it isn't important."

He dragged his eyes away from Allison. "Forgive me. I'm being rude."

"Distracted." She patted his hand. "But I'll let it go this time. What I said was I believe your young lady has charmed Preston. Not an easy accomplishment."

"It isn't, is it?" Ian glanced at Allison again.

The woman's smile turned knowing. "Tell me about her. You can't seem to keep your eyes off her. I don't recognize her from the newspapers."

"She works for me. She's the engineer overseeing the repairs to the castle."

"My, she must be smart and accomplished to have that much responsibility."

Most of his thoughts lately had centered on his body's reaction to her. "She's smart."

"Not your usual 'looks good, no brains kind of woman'." She studied him.

Ian chuckled. "Have they all been that bad, Lucinda?"

"Not if you didn't have to speak with them."

Ian laughed and observed Allison once more. "I can say she's interested in more than herself."

Allison grinned. Under the table, she briefly squeezed his knee.

Ian's attention returned to Lucinda.

"And one of those *interests* is you, would be my guess." The older woman's eyes twinkled.

Their tablemates stood, preparing to leave. Ian hoped he was presentable after Allison's attention. "Lucinda, it's always a pleasure to see you. Allison promised to review plans for Alfred Winters before we go."

They spent the next twenty minutes in the Winters' suite of the hotel going over the plans for his manor house with the crumbling foundation. She overwhelmed Ian with her knowledge and confidence as she discussed the drawings with the older man.

"Young lady, I have to say you've impressed me. I hope you submit a bid to do the work."

"I'm sorry, I won't be doing any onsite work in the future. My firm's hiring someone to handle that soon. If you would still like a bid, I'll see that you have one, but it may be a few months before we could start the work."

"I understand, and that would be fine." Winters looked pleased with himself. He turned to Ian. "Hartley, if you're smart enough to have someone of this caliber working for you, then I think I can trust you with my business. Send over your proposal, and I'll give it a look."

Excitement coursed through Ian as he extended his hand. "Thank you, sir. You'll have it tomorrow."

"Very good."

As Ian drove away from the hotel, he squeezed Allison's hand, "You were quite something tonight. I've never seen Westworth so civil. And with Winters, you were nothing short of brilliant. I've worked for months to have him look at my proposal."

"You're welcome. Just me being me. I learned long ago that if you talk about something a man's interested in, it always makes him like you." She grinned and gave him a knowing glance.

Ian's gaze met hers. "I know other things you do having nothing to do with business that make me appreciate you."

"What? Falling on the ground while chasing a

lamb? Wearing wild toenail polish? Having a pink hardhat?" Allison wrapped her hand around his arm and grinned.

Ian gave her a quick kiss on the forehead. "Those too, but I had something else in mind."

Had he ever been happier? If so, it was long ago. Too long ago. He looked at Allison with her head resting on his shoulder. She made the difference. Challenged him, made him question his decisions. Allison was good for him.

Sometime later he woke her.

"Where are we?" Allison asked looking around the small parking lot.

"The Royal Inn." Ian helped her from the car and directed her toward the door.

"You meant that? I didn't bring a bag." Her voice rose with concern.

"You don't need anything. Of all the people I know you're the most capable of roughing it."

With that, her shoulders straightened. "I can do that."

Ian softly chuckled. Throw a challenge out, and Allison would rise every time. "I don't think this will be too difficult."

Inside the inn, Ian checked them in.

The man handed Ian a key. "Upstairs, to the right, and all the way to the end."

Ian and Allison followed the man's directions. Finally, they came to a wooden door, and Ian slipped the key in the lock. To his surprise, Allison hadn't questioned him further. Until he closed the door behind them.

Amazement glowed on her face as she stood in the middle of the room with her eyes wide.

Everything he'd requested, a blazing fire, with two cushioned armchairs placed in front of it was there. A large four-poster bed stood opposite the grouping with pillows piled against the headboard.

"What a lovely room." The awe in her voice came out slow and sweet.

Ian smiled. He'd made a point of asking for the nicest room and the one furthest from the pub. He wanted privacy.

"What're we doing here, Ian?" Allison sounded unsure.

"I wanted to spend time with you that didn't involve your job or mine, or my family. Just the two of us. For once, I wanted to wake up with you without stealing off in the early morning like a thief in my own home."

"Really lovely speech. Thank you." Allison kissed him on the cheek. "Ooo, I've got to get these heels off." She sat in the nearest chair and kicked her shoes from her feet, wiggling her toes. "I missed my broken-in work boots tonight."

Ian pulled the other chair closer and sat. "I appreciate your sacrifice. Let me see if I can help."

He scooped her legs up and placed them across his thighs. His palm ran along one calf.

Allison shivered and then shifted, pulling her dress higher leaving most of her legs visible. Had Ian noticed? She looked at him from under hooded eyes. His burned brightly. He had. She scooted back as far as the chair would allow giving him access to as much area as possible.

His intense focus remained on the length of skin she'd uncovered. She shifted causing the dress to hike up further. Ian's hard muscle leg flexed beneath hers. A sense of power roared through her with her ability to bring out this type of reaction in Ian. Weeks ago, she wouldn't have dared to act this way. Ian had given her that gift.

Ian made a sound low in his throat. "I'd stop wiggling unless you want me to forget about the foot rub and move on to other areas."

She giggled. "Getting hot and bothered, my lord?"

"There's that sassy mouth again." Ian rolled his thumbs around, pushing against the bottom of one foot. His long fingers practiced their magic across the top of her foot. The flex and release, pull and push reminded her of the saltwater taffy she'd once seen made, but this was much sweeter.

She sighed.

His hands paused and then moved again across her sensitized skin. Cupping her heel in his palm, he held her foot so that his hand filled the hollows on either side. He ran his other hand over the ridge of her foot, alternating pressure as she registered each subtle shift of force by his fingers.

"I could stand having this done forever."

His hand hesitated a moment before starting once more.

They hadn't talked about the future. His hesitation told her that Ian avoided forever. Her heart ached at the idea. But wasn't that their agreement? After all, she had plans she'd worked years to achieve. She didn't deviate from her plans.

Laying her head against the chair, Allison slid into a reclining position. She enjoyed his manipulations and lowered her eyes in pleasure.

Ian's fingers glided over the tops of each toe,

before he tugged on first the big one, continuing until he reached her baby toe that begged for the same attention.

A purr of delight passed her barely parted lips. A groan of protest followed when Ian set that foot down. The idea of more delights built when his care moved to the other foot. He gave this one the same consideration he had given the first.

Oh, the man had the touch!

Finished with the last toe, Ian lifted her leg. Her eyes clouded with desire. In the time it took her to wonder what he'd planned; she felt the coolness of his lips on her calf. A quiver of desire shot along her spine. She sucked in a breath as heat flooded her already heated center. Ian understood seduction.

His month made a poof sound as his lips left her skin in the quiet of the room. The spot went from blue flame hot to iceberg cold at the loss. His lips returned to travel over her skin to the interior of her thigh. A hot stream of need raced to her center, pooled and pulse.

Before she could recover, Ian's teeth nipped her skin. She jerked. One of his hands continued to hold her ankle in a tender but firm grip, while the other palm caressed the underside of her leg inching upwards. She twisted in the chair. Her body like a fire ready to burst into flames.

Ian's eyes remained hooded as he smiled at her. The sexy, wolfish movement of his lips captured Allison's soul, branding it his.

Her heart jumped erratically as he moved higher on her leg, his tongue flicking out to taste her as he went. She squirmed. Could she stand much more?

"You like a foot massage, I see." A note of teasing laced his voice.

"Mmm. Yours."

Finding the small mole high on her thigh Ian covered it with his lips. He looked at her. His smoldering gaze met hers. Her breath caught.

Caught in his web, she took small panting breaths while her heartbeat shifted to streaming speed. Seconds came, went, as their gazes held.

Two could play this game. He had her so hot her center pounded. She wanted him to feel the same. "I'd like to show you my appreciation for the foot rub."

With deliberate movements, she carefully lifted her legs from his thighs and placed her feet on the floor. Standing, she held his gaze as she straddled his legs and sat in his lap, facing him.

Ian's eyes blazed with desire.

She rather liked his attention. Leisurely, she moved until she settled over his groin. He parted his legs, spreading hers wide. Her dress moved high on her hips, leaving her center open. He slid his hand tantalizingly slow up the inside of her leg. He stopped just short of touching her aching need. His expression turned to one of shock. "No panties."

Heat rose to her cheeks. "Clarissa said I couldn't wear any because it ruined the line of the dress."

Ian leaned his forehead against her breasts. His breathing rugged. "I'm glad I'm just now finding out. If I'd known that during dinner, I'd have been witless. And I was already having a difficult time focusing."

She liked that idea of Ian being hot and bother

over her.

"So how do you feel about it now?" She shifted forward then back over his iron-hard length.

His head rose as he caressed her center. "Oh, I think it's incredible."

His finger teased her before sliding into her. The hot lovely feeling that only Ian could create washed throughout her body.

Allison trembled. She wanted this. Wanted him.

She slid back, away from his hand. Reaching the button at his waist, she worked it loose. Carefully she unzipped his pants. Ian was large. She pressed her palm over him. With his underwear out of the away, his manhood stood long and proud between them. She loved that she could make him want her so.

"My trousers..." Ian said, gruffly starting to rise.

"They'll wait. I can't. Condom?"

Ian dug into his trousers' pocket and pulled out a square package. She took it from him, opened it, and rolled the protection on. She then leaned to him, her kisses demanding, deep and wet.

All thoughts of anything but Ian were shoved out of her mind. She wanted him to let go of that control he was so famous for and let her take over. Releasing his lips, she met his gaze and held it. Lowering her center over him, she took him completely.

She didn't move. Ian remained still. Even nicer. Their gaze held. When he started to lift his hips, she placed her hands on his shoulders and calmed him. "My way."

Ian didn't argue.

She flexed her interior muscles, and watched as Ian's eyes widened, then blazed.

He growled, low and feral. "You do that again, and I'll be gone."

Allison couldn't stop the you-dared-me grin from coming to her lips. She lifted her hips to the point he almost slipped out of her and then took him again. His fingers bit into her waist. She flexed once more.

"Allison!" The muscles of his legs tensed. The skin along his jawline tightened, and with his head thrown back he bucked then howled his release.

When he returned to earth, he lifted her off him and carried her to the bed. "You're a wicked, wicked woman."

She giggled. "See, letting go of the control has its advantages."

Mid-morning Ian left the sleeping Allison to go downstairs and order them something to eat. As much as he hated it, they both had to return to work. At one time, his job compartmentalized his life. Now he saw it as more of an interference. Work was time he could be spending with Allison.

He returned quietly to find Allison had moved into the spot he'd vacated. She'd gathered his pillow to her and had it next to her face. Her fiery hair whirled and swirled around her face creating a beautiful picture.

Allison had been something last night. The perfect lover - teasing, tempting, and tantalizing. She'd taken the lead again, driving him out of control. The same as the first time. Allison proved herself correct. The exhilaration of letting go and going along for the ride could add to the pleasure. Heaven knows, the ride with her had been sublime.

He studied her. Why couldn't it be like that every night? Like this each morning? She belonged with him.

Ian placed the mugs he'd brought up on the side table. He sat on the edge of the bed and kissed her temple. He couldn't keep his hands or his lips off her.

Allison moved, rubbing her face against the pillow. Her eyelids slowly opened, and her gaze met his. She gave him a shy smile. He caressed her cheek with the tip of a finger. Taking his hand, she pressed a kiss to his palm.

He returned a tender one to her lips. Wrapping her arms around his neck, she tugged until he came down over her. With a giggle and wiggle of her body she made everything leave his mind. Except having her.

Too soon, moments like these would be gone unless he could find a way to make her stay.

CHAPTER TEN

The next afternoon Allison entered the castle through the hidden side door. Looking up at the detailed woodwork, she thought about how much she loved this old building. She would miss the castle. Ian entered his office from the hallway.

Her heart quickened at the sight of him.

She didn't often sleep late but this morning she had. Ian had come to her bedroom when the castle had quieted, and they had made love again and again. Heaven help her; she was in love with him. Could he possibly love her in return?

Even if he did, would it change things? She had her dreams, and her life mapped out. Could she change enough that he could see her as Lady Hartley material? Was she willing to try? She was. But what if he didn't want her like that? Maybe all he wanted was a sexual relationship until he found the correct woman for his wife. Could she stand to watch that happen?

She understood his need to meet his family

obligations. But would he delegate some of his responsibilities? Could he let go of his ambitions and travel? She thought about her new home—filled with memories—waiting for her.

Good sex and laughter didn't translate into forever.

She would miss the twinkle in Ian's eye and the sexy grin on his face—along with the expression of male satisfaction that came with knowing why she was late that she saw on his lips right now.

Their lovemaking had been both fierce and tender the night before and this morning. Even now, she wanted to crawl into bed with him. She feared how much she cared might showed on her face.

Things had changed between them after their stay at the inn, but neither of them seemed eager to burst the bubble they were in by talking about it. The time for her to leave loomed like a dark cloud. Still, she said nothing, and neither did he.

"Hi, love. What a nice surprise. Looking for me?" He wiggled his brows in a wolfish manner.

She laughed. "Well, not really. But I can't say I'm disappointed to see you."

"In that case..." Ian pulled her tight against him, bringing his mouth to hers in a hot demanding kiss. Allison hung on, enjoying the explosion of emotion within her. She reveled in his desire. The knowledge she created that within him warmed her heart.

Where he once might have tried to hide their relationship days ago, he seemed proud to have it out in the open now. As if making a statement— his castle, his woman— and he wasn't hiding from anyone.

"I've thought of nothing but this for the last hour." Ian's rough voice filled her ear. Circling his waist with her arms, she pulled him tight.

"It's nice to know you've thought of me," she purred against his neck before placing tiny kisses along his jaw on the way to his lips.

His hands crawled under her tee and slid over her flesh along her ribs and stopped to cup her breasts.

A sound somewhere in the castle made them break apart.

Ian continued to hold her hand. "I think we'll have to make this wait until tonight. By the way, I promised to take Jonathan over to the McGregor farm this afternoon. Do you want to go along?"

"I'd love it, but I have a phone call with a contractor coming up."

"We'll wait," Ian assured her.

"Okay. I'll come to your office when I'm done."

"Good." Ian gave her a quick kiss and stepped away.

She would miss this when she was gone. A sadness settled over her. She had to start breaking away, but she'd do that after going to the McGregor farm. After tonight in Ian's bed. After she went home.

Ian took Allison's hand as they walked up the lane, and the children ran ahead of them. Something about the moment felt right. What would it be like to walk across the fields with Allison watching their own children run ahead of them? That idea made him nervous.

He'd thought he'd found the right woman once

before, and his marriage turned into a complete disaster. He'd even hoped that a few women he'd dated would be the right one. Instead they had been the type of women who put their needs first, and found his social and financial status more important than him. Allison was nothing like them. She'd no interest in either. He liked that about her.

So much so he'd left Hong Kong to come home to see her. After his departure, one of the lawyers had found a problem. A mad scramble ensued and it took three days to sort it out. The personal touch was still needed even in this modern world. He'd racked his brain for days now on how he could continue to stay at the castle and keep the business growing? He put aside that thought for now.

Allison had turned his life upside down, and he needed it right side up. Everything in its place.

"Wait up," he called. "I need to show you where to go through the fence."

The kids stopped. He and Allison caught up with them. As he opened the small, almost hidden gate, she stayed with the kids. Margaret put her hand in Allison's as they walked through the opening. He showed Jonathan how to close the gate.

Their group strolled across the field toward the McGregor's farm in the valley. Again, the kids ran ahead as he and Allison came more slowly. Even for him, the picture was pastoral. He didn't often make the effort to enjoy time off in the middle of the day. Before Allison came along, he never would have.

She seemed quieter than usual, even a little pensive.

"Hey, what're you thinking over there?" He gave her hand a gentle squeeze.

She didn't answer immediately. When she did, a note of sadness tinged her voice. "I was thinking how much I love this country. I've worked all over the world, but this might be one of my very favorite places. Next to my grandparents' home."

The one she'd wrap her life plan around. The place that would take her away from him. That wasn't correct. He'd be letting her go. He hadn't asked her to stay. What could he offer her?

Him working day and night. Nights spent alone. Him putting the company before her. Restricting her with Lady Hartley duties. He wouldn't do that. Couldn't take way the free spirit that made her who she was.

He brought Allison against him. Before letting her go, he kissed her forehead. "We'd better pick up our pace, or the kids will reach the McGregor farm before we do."

Mr. McGregor waited in the barnyard for their arrival. Ian had called ahead to let them know they would like to visit.

"Aye, I see you brought your lady friend as well." Mr. McGregor greeted him in a gruff voice and with a handshake.

Allison smiled broadly. "He couldn't keep me away."

Ian introduced Jonathan and Margaret.

"The lambs are over in a pen," Mr. McGregor led them to the side of the barn.

"Can we pet one?" Jonathan asked.

"Yes." They all went into the pen.

The adults stood to the side, watching as the children moved from lamb to lamb.

"There are pups if you would like to see them,"

Mr. McGregor said after the children returned to them.

They jumped around him. "Yes, yes."

"Careful with the puppies. Bessie, their mum's, very protective." Mr. McGregor said with a twinkle in his eye.

Ian glanced at Allison and found her as engrossed by the animals as the kids.

"I can hardly wait to see them again. I beat they have really grown" Allison went and stood between the children taking their hands. "We'll be easy, won't we, kids?"

They both nodded.

Mr. McGregor opened the shed door, and they entered. The shuffle and yelps of active puppies filled the air. Bessie sat near the small pen holding her family.

"Can we hold one?" Jonathan pleaded.

Mr. McGregor nodded. "Sit there." He pointed to a bench. "Very careful now, not to drop them. Hold them gently."

Both children sat obediently, Allison next to them. "My favorite's the black and gold one."

Mr. McGregor handed each of the children a pup and then to Allison the one she requested.

The same rapture that appeared on the children's faces came to Allison's. She brought the small animal up to her cheek. What would it feel like being on the receiving end of her love and devotion? Like basking in warm sunlight.

Bessie started to circle the space. Mr. McGregor said, "It's time to put Bessie's pups down. They need to eat."

The children reluctantly handed Mr. McGregor

the young dogs. Allison placed a kiss on the head of the puppy she held before handing it back. They left the barn and headed inside the McGregor home, where Mrs. McGregor had cookies and milk waiting.

Half an hour later, he and Allison walked behind the children on their return trip to the castle.

Allison sighed deeply and hugged his arm. "This has been the best afternoon ever. I vow to make sure I have more like them. You should too."

He didn't see how that could happen. His lifestyle and the demands of his job didn't leave time for such. And Allison wouldn't be there. Even now, he needed to get to the castle for a video conference.

And then he'd have to learn to let her go.

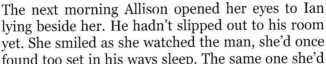

The next morning Allison opened her eyes to Ian lying beside her. He hadn't slipped out to his room yet. She smiled as she watched the man, she'd once found too set in his ways sleep. The same one she'd said she didn't even like when they met. He could still frustrate her with his unbending ways and unwavering focus on work. But she also understood, it was his way of showing love. He did it for his family. She could count on him to make a choice and stand by it.

These thoughts ran though the mind of a woman in love. One whose heart would weep when she left. And leave she must. Ian had said nothing about their future or his feelings or anything about love. But every look, touch, and action, he left her no doubt he cared. Yet their days together were ending.

The tower repair had come to an end. The masons would place the last of the stone on the truants today. The only hurdle left was the inspector's review to see if the repairs met regulations. That visit had been scheduled for the day after tomorrow. Unless something unforeseen happened, she'd leave two days later.

Ian sighed softly. Glancing to see if he was awake, she saw a flicker of his eyelids and a tiny movement at the corner of his lips. Her fingers glazed over the hair that blanketed the plane of his chest.

With the speed of a mousetrap, Ian's hand caught hers between his warm one. "You shouldn't mess with a man while he's sleeping. You never know if he'll wake up mad."

"Oh," she cooed, "I'm not worried about that." She pulled her hand from his, sliding it across his chest as she enjoyed the flex and pull of the muscles beneath her fingers. Dipping lower, she followed the trail of hair that led beneath the sheet.

He flipped, pinning her beneath him. The blue of his eyes deepened as he brought his mouth lower to take hers in a hungry kiss.

Soon, Allison rested in Ian's arms and watched the rainbow of color play across the bedcovers as it streamed through the cut glass of the window.

"You know this could become a habit for me," Ian murmured as his hand traveled back and forth over her bare hip.

Allison's heart skipped. Her hand cupped his cheek. "It's nice."

After quiet moments Ian said, "I'd like you to stay after the tower's finished."

She sucked in a breath. Was this what she'd

been hoping for? She turned to gaze into his eyes. "What're you asking, Ian?"

"I'd like us to spend more time together. Get to know each other better. You could stay with me in London. Travel with me. I could even use your business expertise at times."

Was that what she wanted? She gave him a questioning glance. "So, I'd work for you?"

Ian shrugged a shoulder. "Well, sort of."

Why did he act so evasive? She sat up, putting distance between them. Ian rolled to his side, propping his head on his hand.

"How long? A month? Two? Six? What're you really wanting? A travel partner or a lover? An employee? Someone waiting for your return?"

He seemed perplexed by her questions. "I want you."

Allison's heart tripped. That sounded like a step in the right direction. Still, he hadn't declared his feelings. She took his free hand and played with his fingers as she spoke. "And what does that mean?"

Shadows filled his eyes. "Allison, I care about you."

"And that means exactly what?" The hope in her chest deflated. She shook her head. "I'm sorry, Ian. I want more. I want a place to call home. Marriage. Children. I won't settle for less. I'm done with moving around all the time. I can't settle."

"I'm not the man to give you that."

"Are you sure the word isn't 'won't'?"

"Maybe. I think my life's too restraining for you. I have a traditional family, a name to uphold, where there are certain expectations."

"And I don't fit into those." Once again, she wasn't good enough. Despite all Ian had said, she didn't make the mark. She was good enough for him to take to bed, to introduce to business associates, but not good enough to carry the Hartley name. "Thanks for your honesty."

"It has nothing to do with who you are. You're great. It has everything to do with me. I've responsibilities as the head of the Hartley family, expectations."

"A woman engineer, an American, who wears boots, a pink hardhat, and gets dirt under her nails doesn't fit that mold."

"Allison, you don't—"

"Understand? Yeah, I get it. You gave up your dreams so you could take care of the business and your mother and sister. I've not met your mother, but from what I know about Clarissa they don't need you to hover. Have you thought maybe it's time for you to start living for yourself? I think you're hiding. That you don't want to face what your life has become."

"Like you're going to do?"

"What do you mean?" she asked watching him, her heart pounding.

"You've your life so planned out that you won't bend your plans enough to stay here with me. See what we could have."

"You've already told me what we'd have." She almost spat the words. "Basically, I'd be your mistress. I can see it now. We'd 'date' but the world would understand I'd never become your wife. I might be rigid, but I've some pride. And I know what I want out of life. The bigger question here is—do you know what you want?"

"I don't have the luxury of deciding that. What I have to do was made clear when my father and brother died."

"Maybe so, but could it take a different form from the one you have?" She sighed. "I've spent the better part of my life turning into what my father wanted me to become. The only way I could push against his demands was by being my own person in other ways. I enjoyed my job, but I wore a pink hardhat. I've seen the world, but that's not what I want. Now I need another chance to grow—and to set roots. I think you do too."

"You could do that here with me. You can run your business anywhere. Bake anywhere. It doesn't have to be in America."

"We've come full circle. I'm sorry, Ian, but I want more than you can offer. I won't settle for less. It'd be unfair to me. Or you. We agreed to one night, and foolishly we let it go longer. Let's call it a nice fling, a very nice break from reality, and leave it at that." Allison hated the hurt filling his eyes. The ache in her chest matched it.

"You're asking for promises I can't give."

She didn't say anything for a moment, trying to pick the right words. "I feel sorry for you, Ian. You can't see what you have. Not just me but other things as well. An ancestral home to be proud of. A sister and mother who drive you crazy, but you love deeply. A thriving business. It's what others' dreams are made of, yet you see it as a burden. I hate that for you."

"You don't understand—"

"Apparently, I don't." He reached for her, but she stood and picked up her clothes.

"Allison, I'm sorry if you think I've misled you."

"You haven't." She waved her hand at him. The moisture in her eyes making him a blur. "I'll leave as soon as the final papers are filed," she said softly. "I'd appreciate HRD receiving a good reference. I also think it's best if we have no further contact after that. It'd only make matters more difficult."

Ian rolled to his back and lay with his arm across his face as she quickly dressed. She stood for a moment taking in his beautiful, naked form for one last time before she quietly let herself out the door.

Allison's last two days at Hartley Castle passed with excruciating slowness. As high on the mountain top as she'd lived the weeks before, she now existed in the deepest crevice.

After she'd left Ian the other morning, they'd seen little of each other. For that, she gave thanks. The few times they'd come in contact, she'd wanted to scream touch me, hold me. He'd left the afternoon of the day they had disagreed. She didn't think she'd see him again.

Her pain physically sharpened with that knowledge. She worked by rote because her mind remained on Ian. Even as massive and expansive as the castle was, somehow, her body recognized when he was there. She felt the coldness when he left as if an unnatural force connected them. What would she do when an ocean lay between them?

He cared for her. She didn't doubt that. He'd made love to her too tenderly not to care. Somehow, she'd have to deal with his loss, but she'd never forget him.

The inspector was due in the morning. If he signed off on the work, he would issue a certificate, and Allison's job would be done. She'd already released the work crews, even referring them to Jordon, who would soon start her project near York. The next day she'd made plans to ride the train to the coast where she would meet Mallory and Jordon for a few days.

They'd later join her in America to finalize the company changes and help hire a new engineer to replace her. Life moved on, but somehow, it felt more like it had stopped.

Allison flopped on the bed she and Ian had shared so many times. She stared at the hundreds of years old smoke-darkened beams. She'd miss the stone fortress almost as much as Ian. Not since childhood had the thought of leaving a place brought tears.

Her phone rang. Roger informed her the inspector had arrived. His visit would be the final stamp on her time spent with Ian.

The inspector pronounced the reconstruction historically accurate and livable. With the certificate of clearance now in her hand, sadly nothing kept her at Hartley Castle. After wishing the inspector a good day, she stopped by Roger's office.

"I know my plans were for me to leave tomorrow, but I'd like to leave in the next hour. Would you mind giving me a ride to the train station?"

Roger paused before he spoke. "Are you sure that's what you want to do? Ian's due back this evening."

"I think it's for the best. There's nothing more for me to do here. I'll say my goodbyes and join my friends a day early." For once, owning the minimum of clothing would be a plus.

"Would you please see that Ian gets this?" She handed him the papers from the inspection.

Roger's eyes filled with concern. "Why don't you wait and see him before you go?"

Allison fumbled with the papers. "I don't think so. If there are any problems or questions, he can contact the office."

"I don't know what happened between you and Ian or why, but I do know he's more like his old self since you've arrived."

Allison gave him a watery smile. "I'll miss you, Roger."

He came around the desk and hugged her. She squared her shoulders and went to find Mrs. White. She took Allison's exit much as Roger had. Mrs. White told her, "Dearie, I know you well enough to understand that this is a mistake."

"Mrs. White, you're a love, but I have to go."

She found Clarissa and the children in one of the new rooms in the tower playing a board game. Clarissa's disappointment matched Roger and Mrs. White's. If only Ian believed the same.

CHAPTER ELEVEN

an shoved aside the papers on his London office desk. Shifting in his chair, he put his feet up and rubbed his hands across his face. Sleep hadn't come easily in the past weeks. His work suffered. Since Allison left, nothing seemed to click.

All those long miserable days ago, he'd arrived at the castle from an overnight trip to find Allison gone. *Gone.* The cold hunk of stone had turned freezing once again. With Allison there, the castle turned into a warm and welcoming place. Not anymore. She wanted something he couldn't give. She wanted a place in his life, his name. If it were just him to consider, he'd have already married her.

He missed Allison. He carried a constant pain in his chest. He couldn't soothe it by working. He'd even tried dating. What a disaster. He wanted Allison, needed her. Needed her way of looking at things. Needed her to remind him he didn't control everything in his life and couldn't if he wanted to. He needed her to add that extra spice to his life.

He wanted what he'd felt when she was with him. Wanted her presence after a horrible day. Wanted the wonder she added to his world. Wanted her in his arms. He moaned like a wounded dog. Somehow, he'd get beyond these feelings.

The next day he reluctantly headed to the castle at the request of Clarissa for a weekend reunion with her and their mother. She wanted to visit to see how the repairs had turned out. When he arrived at the castle, his mother greeted him in the great hall, looking youthful and perfectly dressed as ever. He had to admit she was still an attractive woman.

She hurried to him with open arms. "Hello, sweetheart."

"Hi, Mum." He brought his mother into a hug and kissed her on the cheek. He checked beyond her for one of her new men, but to his surprise, there was none.

She pushed him away, studying him. "You look awful."

"Thank you. That's what a child always wants to hear from his mother."

She patted him on the cheek. "You grew into a man a long time ago. That's part of your trouble."

After his father and brother died, he'd had to grow up fast. It wasn't until Allison had pushed him to laugh that he'd felt young again.

"One of us had to be the adult."

His mother wagged her finger at him. "Watch it. I'm still your mother."

Yes, and a wonderful one. Open, caring, and attentive. Why had he forgotten that?

"Clarissa's had nothing but glowing things to

say about the new rooms and the work that has been done. I'd love a tour."

Ian had avoided the tower since Allison had left. He wasn't enthusiastic about the idea now. "I guess now is as good a time as any."

His mother gave him a questioning glance but didn't comment before she started toward the stairs. Half an hour later, they came back down.

"Well, it looks like your contractor did a wonderful job. I couldn't tell where the old ended, and the new began."

His contractor. Allison had been his, and he'd let her go. Since when did his mother pay attention to anything like building construction? Had Clarissa told her about him and Allison? "Yes, the contractor was excellent."

"I heard she was nice. Clarissa liked her." His mother's eyes narrowed. "And that you did too."

His mother had no idea how much. "She did a fine job. I wish all the jobs I contracted went as quickly and turned out so successfully."

His mother stopped and considered him. "What's that I hear in your voice?"

Sadness, disappointment, loneliness? He sounded pathetic. Somehow, he needed to get a handle on his life again. Ian cleared his throat. "There's nothing wrong with my voice."

"Who're you trying to convince, you or me? I understand you and Allison became close."

"Clarissa talks too much." Ian turned to leave.

"You wait a minute. I'm her mother, as well. She tells me things." He faced his mother. "And she's concerned about you. I think she's right. You do look...tired and unhappy."

"I'm a busy man with responsibilities." Sometimes he wondered if his mother had a clue what his day-to-day life consisted of as she wandered the world spending money and picking up men.

"I know you do, but some of those are self-imposed."

That statement irritated him. The best he could tell most of them had been dumped in his lap. "What exactly does that mean?"

"You've worked hard to run the business, to take care of us, and honor your father. I appreciate that, but you have allowed work take over your life."

"Who would do it, if I didn't?" he spat.

She placed a hand on his arm. "We could sell the company or hire people to manage it. Head the board and do what you'd like to do."

Ian gave her an incredulous glare. "That'd be okay with you?"

"Yes. I hate how the business has consumed your life. I want you to have a life. Someone to love, children, happiness. We'll all be Hartleys whether or not you're head of Hartley Shipping."

"Why haven't you said something before?"

"Would you have listened?"

"Probably not." Ian hung his head. They'd never talked about business before.

His mother studied him. "I see she's changed you for the better. Honey, the way you have lived isn't how your dad lived. Isn't what your dad would've wanted for you to have a life you enjoyed. Somewhere along the line, you chose to quit living. You've spent your time working and feeling obligated to the family too long. You have forgotten to take time for yourself. You even chose the wrong person because you thought she would make the right Mrs. Hartley. That's no way to have a marriage." Her eyes softened, and her mouth took on a wry smile as she cupped his cheek again. "It's time you decide what you want out of life. Find your one true love. I had your father. I want that for you. Open yourself up. Take a chance. You can't control everything or everyone. Don't wait until it's too late." She stepped back. "Think about it. Now, I'm going to see what Mrs. White has planned for my homecoming dinner and catch up on the local gossip."

His mother walked toward the kitchen. She left him with a great deal to think about.

The next day he sat in his office at the castle trying to get some much-needed work completed, but instead, his mother's words kept running through his mind. Was she correct?

Had he been so wrapped up in the Hartley image, protecting the name and business that he'd stopped living? Given up his dreams? Could he even remember what he used to dream?

One answer became crystal clear. He wanted Allison in his life full time and forever. He intended to tell her that he wanted a partnership with her, if she would only have him. Take a chance on him.

He called Roger. "I want the plane ready to go in two hours."

"I'll need to give them a destination, so they can file a flight plan," Roger said.

"Huntsville, Alabama."

"I'll let the pilot know." Roger's voice held a sound of amusement. "Tell Allison I said hello."

"I will if she'll speak to me."

"She will."

With all his heart, Ian hoped so. "I've an errand to run before I leave. I'll return in about an hour."

Allison sat at her new desk in the small bedroom of her grandparents' house, now her house. Her grandparents were happily situated in a retirement village. She'd achieved her dream, but the joy she'd anticipated was missing. Someone who mattered more was missing. Ian. With her chin in the palm of her hand, she stared out the window at nothing. The sun shone bright, but she didn't care if the rain poured. Her mind wandered to thousands of miles away.

Alabama had been home for over a month. Mallory and Jordon had complained she was no fun during their getaway. Allison had agreed, and left three days early to come home to nurse her aching heart.

The flight home matched her unsteady turbulent emotions. Her greatest fear had happened. Leaving Ian had broken her heart. Destroyed her soul.

The nights were the worst. She'd slept little since leaving Hartley Castle and Ian's arms. What rest she got came in the early hours, but only after she had tossed and turned. She missed curling against the warm length of him. As if her body had become addicted to his.

Allison had often wondered what lovesick meant, and now she felt it's sting. She hardly ate. She went through the motions of working, trying to sort their upcoming projects and bid on others while setting up the home base. Each day the mental fog wouldn't clear. With her grandparents' house hers and the COO position transitioning, she had everything she'd worked and planned for. Yet she had nothing.

The reconnection with her family hadn't eased the pain. Since her parents now lived in the Huntsville area, she had a chance to see them regularly. Her brother from Colorado and sister from Florida and their young families had come for a long-weekend visit to welcome her home. The reunion had been wonderful, but it didn't fill her with the joy she'd hoped for. The one person who could do that and put her out of her misery was thousands of miles away. Nothing would ever replace Ian. Not her family, her grandparents' house or her memories.

She exhaled and pushed back from the desk to head to the kitchen. She'd always baked as an outlet for her emotions. These days she overused her skill. She pulled out the ingredients to make bread. Kneading the fresh dough, adding flour to the sticky mass, gave her control in her life. After a week she'd had loaves and loaves of bread stacked in her kitchen. So many she had donated the extra to a soup kitchen. She sighed. Today she'd add more to the pile.

Allison had just set the dough to rise when the buzzing of her laptop caught her attention. She glanced at the clock. It was time for her weekly meeting with Mallory and Jordon. Jerking a cloth off a hanger, she wiped her hands as she hurried to the office.

She opened the app and her friend's faces came into view. "Hey, I'm here. Just mixing dough."

"Why am I not surprised?" Jordon quipped.

Mallory leaned in close to the screen. "You look

awful. Have you been bathing? Eating?"

How was she supposed to answer that? She had died inside. "I'm fine."

Jordon studied her and Allison moved back, not wanting them to see the shadows under her eyes. "You're lying. You're going to have to let it go."

Jordon knew that all too well. She carried the scars of disappointment from years ago.

"I'm sorry you're so unhappy," Mallory offered.

Allison's chest tightened. She hated to hear her friends worry over her. "It's nothing that time won't fix."

"Yeah, you should be happy with your new house, a chance to bake all day, and being a paper pusher, while Mallory and I are out doing all the manual labor," Jordon added with a grin.

"Funny," Allison found little humorous these days.

"Seriously, I'm the last one to encourage you to do something that might hurt you more, but have you told him how you feel?" Mallory delivered her question in a calm, even tone.

"From what you've told us, Ian loves you." For Jordon, it was that simple. "Someone has to say it first. Has to be willing to take the first step. Find a compromise."

Allison wished it was that easy. She'd be pushing against hundreds of years of history. "We're so far apart in our ideals that it'll never work. I can't change into what he needs, and he can't bend enough to see he could follow a new path."

"Then make him see it," Mallory insisted.

Jordon's face turned determined. "Have you

ever had a piece of stone that you thought wouldn't go into a spot? Yet you managed to make it work and the wall turned out perfectly?"

Allison nodded.

"Maybe you're a bit rigid about how you have to have things." Jordon took a breath. "You said you loved the castle and the surrounding countryside. You say you love Ian. You can do your COO job from anywhere...maybe your daddy's trait of having it all his way has rubbed off on you."

Allison took a deep breath and held it. Had she done that? Could she change? Be what Ian needed in a Lady Hartley? "What if being with him meant me giving up my partnership?"

Mallory and Jordon looked stricken for a moment. Mallory spoke first. "The firm is important, but it'll never be more important than your happiness."

Jordon's eyes held concern, but she nodded her agreement.

Allison looked back at Mallory, and she nodded. With tears in her eyes, Allison said, "I love you both."

As soon as their call ended, Allison started forming a plan to talk to Ian. When she saw him, she'd start by apologizing for leaving without saying goodbye and work her way to telling him she would do whatever it took for them to find a life together for as long as possible.

First, she'd call Roger and find out Ian's location. When she finished the bread, she'd head out and buy a new suitcase. A nice one to use when she traveled with Ian.

A few hours later, she pulled the last of the loaves from the oven. Allison lifted her arm to rub her nose against her shirt sleeve. Her grandmother had always said that when your nose itches, someone's coming to see you. Allison grinned. Was Ian's nose itching?

As she placed the last pan of rolls in the oven, the doorbell rang. Allison picked up the dishrag, wiped her hands, and dusted off the front of her t-shirt and shorts. She wasn't expecting anyone.

After looking through the glass panel of the front door, her heart slammed against her chest wall. Her hands shook. *Ian. Here.* She'd dreamed of this moment but never thought it would happen.

Just the thought of seeing him again stole her breath. He wore her favorite blue polo shirt and dark tan slacks. All suave male. He looked good enough to eat. Despite his casual dress, he'd stand out anywhere. An expression she'd never seen before shown on his face. Was it fear?

Allison glanced down at her too-causal clothes. Flour clung to her and powered her hair. She looked awful.

The bell rang again. She couldn't leave him standing out there. Allison reached for the doorknob. Her hand slipped. She wiped the dampness from her palm on her shorts then tried again.

"Hello, Allison."

His deep voice with the beautiful accent rolled over her. She made a sound that might have been considered a response. Her knees shook and she held the doorframe to support herself.

He grinned, but not his usual poised one. This man who headed an international company looked unquestionably nervous. She offered him a watery smile.

His insecurity instantly left his face, replaced by a huge smile. He watched her a moment then said quietly, "May I come in?"

She couldn't answer. Instead, she stepped away from the door, allowing him space.

Ian dwarfed the small living area. He checked out the room, newly done in purples, lime green, and red. His eyes lingered on the large painting hung on the wall of a whimsical medieval scene, prominently featuring a castle. One that looked remarkably like Hartley Castle.

"I hadn't expected you," she blurted.

"Whatever happened to that famous southern hospitality?" He stepped toward her. Taking her hand, he gave it a gentle tug, bringing her to him.

Allison could no more resist him than she could a wonderfully made pastry.

Ian ran his hands up her arms making her insides feel like goo before he gathered her closer. His head dipped and his lips took hers in a hungry kiss.

Allison stretched on tiptoes and returned his passion. Everything she'd been missing she communicated through her lips. Her hands followed the breadth of his shoulders until her fingers slipped beneath the hair at his nape. She held his mouth to hers, purring her pleasure. Sinking into pure bliss.

Ian released her. He breath coming out as heavily as hers. "We need to talk while I can still think."

She would've rather continued what they were doing, but she agreed with Ian. They needed to talk. She moved to stand beside a chair across the room. "Okay."

Ian sighed and took a seat on the small sofa, resting his arms on his legs and clasping his hands between his knees. "Would you sit beside me?"

She wasn't too sure about that idea. "I think I'd better sit over here." She took a chair opposite him.

Ian shrugged, grinning. "Roger said you called."

"So instead of returning the call, you decided to drop by? How lordly of you."

"That's one of the many things I love about you. You don't mind saying what you think."

Allison's blood hummed through her veins. He'd said love! But then it could just be a figure of speech. "I called because—"

He held up a hand. "Let me go first."

Lord Hartley in the flesh. He still had to have the upper hand. But she didn't care, she loved that he sat close. She was thrilled to see him. "Okay."

"I don't blame you for leaving. The past month without you has been the worst of my life. I can't concentrate at work. I can't think of anything but you. The people who work for me have stopped talking to me because I'm such a bear. Clarissa told me to stay away from the children until I wised up. I need you, Allison. I need you in my life. To make me laugh. To tell me the truth. To hold you at the end of the day, to make it the best part of the day."

Allison blinked, trying to keep the moisture in her eyes under control. "I need you too. I love you. I was coming to tell you. I want to find a compromise where we can be together. I know you don't think I'm what you need, but I can change—"

"Never said that. I'd never ask you to change." He started toward her.

She stopped him with a hand up. "Hear me out. I've always lived with a plan for my life. A goal. The only way I knew to feel like I had some control over my life was to be quirky in my dress and speak my mind. I even had to own my own company. I know that isn't the type of woman you're looking for. I want to try to be that person. I've spoken to Mallory and Jordon, and they're willing to let me out of my partnership."

Ian shook his head.

"I can hang up my hardhat and put away my boots. I'll even learn to dress more conservatively. I can't do anything about my pedigree, but I can promise to do my best never to embarrass you—at least not on purpose."

"What you must think of me." Such sorrow threaded his words. Ian came to her and gently brought her into his arms. His kiss was tender and loving. "I would never ask you to give up your company for me. Or change how you dress or act or have you watch what you say. I love you just the way you are."

"But, Ian—"

"I was so wrong to suggest that you wouldn't make the perfect Lady Hartley. There's no one else who can fill that position. You're the only one for me. I've been so caught up in upholding the Hartley name I've forgotten what it's like to be a living breathing person. You reminded me of how that felt." He lifted her chin so she could see his eyes. "*Nothing* will ever be more important than you. I'm the one who isn't good enough for you. Please say you forgive me for making you feel anything but perfect. I love you with all my heart."

Allison cupped his cheeks and kissed him.

"You've said all I need to hear. All I've ever wanted from you is your love."

"I'll work every day to deserve it. Since you came into my life, I've looked forward to the future. Hartley Castle became a warm place to come home to because of you."

Allison kissed him again, unable to say anything.

"I've already started moving people into place to run Hartley Shipping. I'm stepping down from running the day-to-day business and plan to head the board. Which means I'll spend most of my time at Hartley Castle overseeing a program of environmental studies and sustainable farming. I want a home, children, and most of all you. Will you be my wife?"

"Ian, are you sure that's what you want? I can change some, but I don't know if I'll ever be the sedate, sit-in-the-corner wife that Lord Hartley needs."

"I'd be disappointed if you were. I want a partner. You are that person. Allison, you're happiness for me. I know with you I can make a marriage work."

"Are you sure?"

"I've never laughed, been as angry or happy or proud, or felt more alive than with you. I know you want a home and children. You can have that with me at the castle, in London, or even here. Wherever you want. We'll make it work. Just as long as you're willing, and you love me."

She threw her arms around him. "There's nothing I want more."

Ian's heart soared. He lifted her into his arms,

holding her tight. "I know how much you enjoy your time in the kitchen. I spoke to Mrs. White and Edna. They assured me they'd gladly share their kitchens with you. If that won't do, we'll buy a new place. I want you to be happy." He surveyed the room. "We can even live here if that's what you want."

She giggled. "That would make it pretty hard to oversee your work on the estate."

"Then I'd just have to figure something out."

"How about we visit for holidays like I did as a kid?" She looked at him adoringly.

Ian like that expression. He kissed her. "A sound plan."

"You've made me the happiest woman ever. You're my dream, Ian. I love you."

His chest swelled with contentment. After so many years of emptiness, he felt alive again. Excited about life.

"And I love you with all my heart. You'll become my Lady, won't you?"

"I will. Just try to get away." Her lips found his.

When they broke the long kiss he said, "I have something special waiting for you at the castle. I thought I might need it to sweeten the deal. When I headed this way, I realized that because of the quarantine laws, it was best not to bring him along." He pulled out his phone and found the picture he needed.

"What?" She peeked over his arm at the screen.

She squealed and hugged him. "My favorite of Mr. McGregor's puppies."

Ian smiled broadly. "He's yours if you want him. I remember you saying how much you wanted a dog when you found a home." He put his hands on her waist as he looked into her eyes. "We come as a pair."

"The perfect pair as far as I'm concerned. I love you and him. What's his name?"

"He doesn't have one. I thought you might like to name him. But that can wait. We've more urgent things to do." He pulled her to him again.

"Such as?" She gave him a wide-eyed look of innocence.

"Things like this." His mouth captured hers, then lifted away long enough for him to ask, "Where's your bedroom?"

Some blissful time later, Ian lay back on the bed pillows with Allison snuggled in his arms. Life had righted itself.

One of Allison's hands traveled over his chest. "I can hardly wait to tell Jordon and Mallory we're getting married and that they'll be in a wedding held at a castle."

Ian chuckled. "You already have it planned, do you?"

"Maybe some of it, but none of it matters if you aren't there." She kissed his neck.

"You can count on me showing up. I wouldn't miss it."

"I guess us having a puppy will be a prelude to having children." For once in his life, the idea appealed to him less as an obligation and more of a pleasure. He rather looked forward to sharing the experience with Allison. He rolled with her, his lips moving across hers. Between quick little kisses, he murmured, "I think we should get started on those right away."

Allison's hand circled his neck. She whispered before her mouth joined his, "Let's."

THE END

DESIGNS ON FOREVER

CHAPTER ONE

Mallory Andrews checked the position of her foot. If she could inch out...

She stretched her arm and extended her leg while maintaining her precarious balance as she moved closer to the spot. Her old yoga coach would have preened with pride. Another small twist should do it. This job must be perfect. The tiniest detail needed attention, even if it might killed her.

Scooting her foot from side to side until it remained half-on, half-off the scaffolding plank, she reached toward the rosette near the top of the chapel ceiling of Ashley Manor Hotel in Cornwell, England. A very unladylike word, that her mother would've chastised her for, escaped.

She twirled the paint brush out to the tip of her fingers. Her lips pursed tight in concentration. When the bristles of the brush touched the spot she grinned in success and with relief.

"There," she exhaled.

Mallory shifted her weight back almost in a standing position when her balance failed. The paint brush went flying, landing with a tiny thump on the distant stone floor. She reached to catch herself, before sitting on her bottom– hard.

A gasp filled the air. She peered over the edge of the board.

An impeccably dressed man in suit and tie craned his neck to look at her. She met his gaze. His good looks dazzled her for a moment. His shoulders were wide enough that he looked fully capable of catching her had she fallen.

"Come down here before you kill yourself!" His tone reached that of a coach chastening his player for poor performance. "You've no business mucking around up there."

Annoyed at his scolding Mallory stood and swatted at the dust on her pants before climbing down. As she neared the floor the man asked, "Are you Mallory Andrews?"

Jumping the last six feet, she landed nimbly, and then moved to stand in front of him. "I am. How can I help you?"

"I believe we had a meeting." Scowling he checked an expensive looking silver watch on his wrist. "You should have been expecting me. I'm Evan Townsend."

"I'm sorry." She looked at the ceiling. "I was touching up after the painters this morning and didn't realize you had arrived." She offered him her most polite, professional smile before giving her bottom a final slap creating a cloud of plaster dust. Bending down, she retrieved her favorite paint brush.

The small hairs on the nape of her neck prickled. Evan Townsend's eyes rested where her hand had been against her jeans. Men had ogled her for years especially when she had been on the modeling catwalk. These days she rarely gave their looks any thought. So, why did Townsend's eyeing her backside make her heart trip?

Scowling he checked his pricey time piece again.

Her heart revved another notch as his gaze moved along her body in increments. His appraisal made her blush like a schoolgirl, sending a shiver down her spine.

He stood well over six feet, would be her guess. She herself had grown well above her friends who had called her stork legs in school. But next to Evan Townsend she could have been average height. Worse, his superior manner made him seem loftier.

Trying to regain her composure she volunteered, "I spoke to your grandmother this morning. She said you were coming. I'm sorry I wasn't available when you got here. I had to check the progress here before the workers returned from lunch break."

"Can we talk now?" Impatience, secured by irritation, wrapped his words.

"Sure. Do you mind if we go by my workroom first? I need to put this brush in some thinner."

"That's fine."

Townsend probably had no idea where her workroom was located or he wouldn't be agreeing to join her. Not only had she given him a fright, he seemed annoyed at her for not being right where he had expected she would be. To make matters worse he'd had to come looking for her. They weren't

Susan Carlisle

getting off on the right foot.

As they walked through the arched chapel doors, he asked, "Do you climb around on the scaffolding often?"

Mallory grinned. "Only when I need to check on something. Which is pretty much all the time."

"Then you should know better than to reach out like that. You almost fell. If you had, you would have been seriously injured. Or killed. What were you doing, anyway?"

"Touching up a missed spot."

He turned his head sideways in question. "Why? It couldn't possibly have been visible from the floor."

"I would know it wasn't right. It doesn't matter whether others can't see it or not. It's not only my job, but the foundation of my reputation that no detail, however small, is overlooked."

"Then you should've had one of the workmen take care of it."

She looked over her shoulder. "Why? I was already up there."

He put his hand on her arm stopping her. "As I said, you could've fallen to your death."

Something electric vibrated through her. Partly because of the physical contact, but more from knowing of his concern for her safety. She found it refreshing to have someone other than her business partners worried about her. Years had passed since a male had shown interest in something other than her looks. Yet at the same time it irritated her. He had implied reckless on her part. Even though she'd reassured him she considered the tiniest detail of her job important and spent a great deal of time on scaffolding.

Mallory waved her hand, dismissing her annoyance. "It's no big deal. I'm used to doing touch-up work. This way, Mr. Townsend."

Winding though the gray stone passageways and down a narrow staircase, she led him through the house toward the bottom floor the manor. She walked beneath a stone archway and along a passage. As she went, she trailed a finger across the cool, rough stone and inhaled the musty scent of the oldest foundation of the house, the part that had been a castle hundreds of years earlier.

She loved everything about Ashley Manor. The square turrets, the steep roofs of the additions made through the years, the stale dampness of her workshop, and the slope of the gardens that led to the ocean that battered the rock cliffs.

Entering a small room, she stepped over to a makeshift table composed of tall, rough wooden planks on sawhorses and plunked the paint brush into the tin can of thinner filled with numerous other brushes.

She turned to find him studying her small cluttered, windowless space. His faint sneer indicated it had failed to impress.

The wooden worktable, which accommodated her height, took up most of the area. Tools, wallpaper swatches and the start of a valance were scattered about. Rolls and bolts of various décor material were stacked along the walls and into the corners. Shelves held equipment, and in one corner sat a small table she used as a desk and sewing area.

"Is this the best you could be given for an office? I'll speak to the manager and see if there's another, more spacious room."

She shook her head. "Please don't. This room is fine. It's quiet and out of the way. I often work late at night, and here I don't disturb anyone."

"If that's the way you want it." He scanned the room again. "I think we should find somewhere else to talk. Let's go to my office."

His office? Why did he have an office here in the manor?

"What's going on?" Her voice rose, betraying her alarm. "Your grandmother implied that you were just coming by to check on how the project is progressing."

"Ms. Andrews—May I call you Mallory? I'm afraid there's more to my visit than that." He directed his hand towards the door. "Let's go upstairs."

"If I'm going to be out of pocket for a while, I need to check with my workers first. I have new instructions for them based on my inspection. I'll meet you in a few minutes."

Exhaling impatience he checked his watch a third time. "Very well. I'm staying in the Master's Room, using the sitting area as an office. We can talk without interruption there."

"I'd prefer to meet elsewhere."

His mobile rang. "Yes. Hold a moment." Granite gray eyes focused on her. "I don't. What I have to say doesn't need to be overheard by the staff. I'll expect you there in ten minutes." He put the phone to his ear again, turned and walked out.

She digested her premonition of a discussion she wasn't going to like and hurried back to the chapel to meet with her workers.

At the tentative knock on the door Evan called, "Enter." He returned to his phone conversation as he studied the open laptop sitting on a table he had moved there from under a window across the room. A portable wifi printer sat nearby. He found the file he needed and relayed the information. Ending the call, he glanced towards the door.

Mallory still stood near it. The only way to describe her would be striking, the most beautiful woman he'd ever seen. To make her more interesting he hadn't anticipated finding someone like her up on scaffolding doing manual labor.

Her legs seemed to go on forever. Being a leg man through and through, he found it difficult not to stare. However, he had no intention of getting involved with someone his grandmother had hired to redecorate this failing manor house turned hotel. To get a grip on his thoughts he waved Mallory forward to the full-cushioned loveseat in front of his desk. He remained in the wing-backed chair he'd positioned behind the small writing desk.

Despite his reluctance to continue her work, he had conceded that Mallory had beautifully and comfortably refurnished the entire Master's Room, including the adjoining bedroom. The last time he'd visited Ashley Court it had been horribly run down inside although the exterior remained stately.

It had been ten years since he had last seen it. He and his grandmother's final argument, which led to them going their separate ways, had been over converting Ashley Manor into an exclusive hotel. The manor house had been the last in a long list of reasons he'd left his grandmother's hotel business and her life. Her vision for the family business and his had been poles apart. Evan still couldn't fathom his grandmother's obsession to continue dumping money into this historical building with no hope of a major return on the investment.

When his grandmother's company's board had begged him to review the place and offer insight on how to bring the company back from the edge of bankruptcy he had no choice but to agree. If he didn't stop the hemorrhaging there wouldn't be money left for his grandmother to live her last days in comfort. He owed her that, at the very least. Handling Ms. Mallory Andrews would be his first step toward stemming the flow.

He watched as she floated, the best description he could find to describe the lithe way she crossed the Oriental rug and settled on the loveseat. Enthralled, he shook his head, clearing it enough to speak. "Did you speak to your men?"

"Yes." She pushed at a strand of hair that could only be its natural color because it was such an unusual shade. Somewhere between tawny and sun streaked blond.

"Good. Then we'll get started."

Her blue eyes looked at him expectantly.

"Mallory, I'm well aware my grandmother hired your firm to redecorate, but I'm afraid that we no longer need your services."

She jumped to her feet. Her eyes wild. "Townsend's Notable Hotels has a contract with Historical Restorations and Designs legally obligating the company to allow me to complete the project as agreed upon. Besides, your grandmother said nothing about terminating this job when I spoke with her this morning. In fact, we discussed some new ideas I have."

Though not being known for tact, Evan attempted a calming tone by lowering his voice. "Please sit down and I'll explain.

He waited until she complied by perching on the edge of the couch, looking as if she would spring again at any wrong word.

"My grandmother's health has been failing over the last few months." Or so he had been told by associates. He'd not seen her ten years either.

Mallory's look of concern assured him that she would at least listen, although her jaw remained tight. He chose his words with care. "I was asked to evaluate your progress and decide what needs to be done to complete the project under budget or to find a good stopping place as soon as possible. I'm aware you've invested a great amount of time into this job. However, I'm not convinced that more of your time or my grandmother's money is necessary. You've done wonders with the rooms I've seen. But to be frank, I don't think enough people will be willing to pay the necessary high prices to justify the maintenance costs. They'll stay in less expensive hotels located nearby. With no return on the already vast investment, it's questionable if we can remain open." He leaned back in his chair. "I tried to get my grandmother to understand this years ago."

From the way she studied him he could tell Mallory had figured out who he was. "You're *that* Evan Townsend. Of Townsend Inns."

Her tone implied she believed he and his inns were beneath contempt. "I am. Have you ever stayed at one of my inns?"

"Yes. Once."

He took her tone to mean that once had been

enough. "You didn't enjoy your stay?"

"I found it a little sterile for my taste."

"Really?" He leaned forward and put his elbows on the desk.

"The same economical style bed in an impersonal room, in every town, in every country. Spending the night away should be better or at least equal to your bedroom at home. When people stay at Ashley Court it'll be an experience to remember, not a feeling of having rented a section of a production line."

Evan blinked. That was harsh. "Some people like knowing what to expect in a hotel. My rooms are affordable."

"You're right. Sadly, for some people your inns are all they can afford. I'll say you do employee an excellent staff."

"Thank you for that at least." He let his mouth twitched at the corner for a second before he turned solemn again.

"However, others want a relaxing experience when they travel. Your grandmother understands that. All her hotels are wonderfully unique, overnight adventures. I've made it a point to stay in one whenever I travel."

"I do appreciate your passion for my grandmother's hotels, but that doesn't change the fact that this one is unacceptably over budget. The question is: Are the renovations fiscally feasible? If they aren't..." He let the other unspoken option dangle between them. "I'd like to see all your expense reports and invoices. And I'll be approving any future spending in advance." He had no intention of arguing over the issue.

"I have orders already placed. I'm expecting

deliveries today."

Apparently, Mallory wasn't going to make this simple. "We'll look at those orders together as soon as possible and determine whether to keep them or return them."

"Mr. Townsend—"

"*Evan.*"

"Evan." She repeated his name as if it had a sour taste. "The suppliers and I have developed a relationship. I can't just return willy-nelly. I've a reputation to uphold. HRD does as well."

"I'm aware. Unfortunately, as of now I'm responsible for making sound financial decisions in regard to this hotel. My fiscal responsibilities overrule your professional pride."

She stiffened more with each of his words, which drew his attention to her T-shirt, stamped with the HRD logo, tightening across her breasts. She had all the right assets. He brought his gaze back to hers.

After taking a deep breath, she said in a terse tone, "I need to finish a number of rooms. May I wrap those up?"

"How many are involved?"

"Ten."

His elbows went to the desk as he intertwined his fingers and rested his chin on them. "With those complete I'd have twenty available to let. Which rooms? All I've inspected appear complete."

"Three need pictures, others pillows and rugs. I've a special chest of drawers ordered for one. All those items should arrive today or tomorrow. Another five rooms are in the process of being papered, having bath fixtures installed. A couple needs beds, chairs, etc."

"As I've said when the items arrive let me know. I'd like to inspect the sale invoices before accepting delivery. I do need more rooms available. The hotel must look like a viable piece of property."

"Viable?" Her voice rose as she leaned towards him, gripped the edge of the desk with both hands. "Are you planning to sell Ashley Court?"

"I'm considering it but that remains to be seen. In any event costs must be cut immediately. If the hotel doesn't appear to be doing a brisk business no one will want to purchase it if I do decide the best course is to put it on the market."

She stood. "You can't do that! It would kill your grandmother. She loves this place."

"I'm all too aware of that. Please sit down, Mallory." She certainly felt passionate about the hotel and her work. Did that extend to other areas of her life?

She lowered to the sofa once more sitting as if she had a rod in her spine.

Why would selling the hotel matter so much to her? He leaned toward her. "When I agreed to do the evaluation I made it clear to the board that selling might be necessary. This place is bleeding my grandmother's other hotels dry. Slowly killing her company. I'll gladly sell it to keep the company from bankruptcy."

"She hasn't said anything about there being a problem."

"I'm sure that's true. You're not the only one with pride. She's always been a bit of a dreamer. She's never understood that pouring more money after good money into a dinosaur of a building isn't a sound business practice."

"But you have." Her words had an accusatory bite to them.

Weary of the conversation he announced, "If the manor is sold, your company will be compensated for the breach of contract. You'll be well paid. I'll also see to it that you and your firm receive positive recommendations. I have some influence in the hotel business world and I'll gladly pass along your name to anyone looking to do renovations."

He glanced around the room. "By the way, are you responsible for decorating this room?"

She nodded her gaze fixated on him.

"Very nice. I like the hunting motif. It works will for Ashley Manor. Do you know that many of the royal family have stayed here?"

Her proud eyes pierced him, rendering him immobile. "I do my homework. I've been working on this project for over six months. I understand Ashley Manor and the history surrounding it down to the finest detail. You apparently have no idea I'm a professional with an excellent education and the hard work experience to back the title up."

"You do such a nice job maybe you would consider coming to work for me if Ashley Manor is sold."

Her chin shifted forward, blue eyes snapping. "Doing what?"

"Furnishing the new Townsend Inn that I'm building in Glennshire."

She expelled a sound of disgust. Holding her feelings in check were obviously foreign to her. What she thought came out. Seeing her reactions over the next few days could make staying at the manor enjoyable. Normally, he wasn't a betting man, but her brand of beauty, brains, and grit made an interesting trifecta that might be worth exploring.

"I'll think about it." She stood slowly. "If we're done here, I've work to do. I'll let you know when the truck arrives."

"Please remind your workers of safety procedures and leave your paperwork on my desk if I'm not here."

She nodded curtly. "My workers are aware of the safety issues."

"Good, then you understand you're not to go up again without a harness."

She glared at him then turned to leave.

Her long sleek arms swung at her sides as she glided with a stiff back toward the door. Her heel to toe placement added extra flair to her tantalizing hip movement. Making her mad every time they met might not be a bad idea if he got to watch her walk away from him. Too much of that pleasure though might drive him mad with desire.

Books by Susan Carlisle

Medical Romances for Harlequin
Heart Surgeon, Hero...Husband?
The Nurse He Shouldn't Notice
Hot-Shot Doc Comes to Town
NYC Angels: The Wallflower's Secret
Snowbound With Dr. Delectable
The Rebel Who Stole Her heart
The Doctor Who Made Her Love Again
The Maverick Who Ruled Her Heart
The Doctor's Redemption
His Best Friends Baby
One Night Before Christmas
Married for the Boss's Baby
White Wedding for a Southern Belle
Doctor's Sleigh Bell Proposal
The Surgeon's Cinderella
Stolen Kisses with Her Boss
Christmas with the Best Man
Redeeming the Rebel Doc
The Brooding Doc Baby Bombshell
A Daddy Sent by Santa
The Sheik Doc's Marriage Bargain
Nurse to Forever Mom
Highland Doc's Christmas Rescue
Firefighter's Unexpected Fling
Second Chances in the South Pacific

Southern Secrets – Novella

Masters of Their Castles Series
Cornerstone of Love
Designs on Forever
Home for His Heart

About the Author

Susan Carlisle's love affair with books began when she made a bad grade in math in the sixth grade. Not allowed to watch TV until she brought the grade up, Susan filled her time with books. She turned her love of reading into a love of writing. Susan has released through HarperCollins's Harlequin medical imprint over twenty-five contemporary romances. Her heroes are strong, vibrant man and the woman who challenge them. She has been a finalist in the Maggie Published and Unpublished, Holt, Gayle Wilson Award for Excellence, and Georgia Author of the Year contests.

As a traditionally published nonfiction author her first book *Nick's New Heart* was released by Tiger Iron Press under Susan May. It is about her son's heart transplant experience. The second, a historical biography *A WWII Flight Surgeon's Story* was released by Pelican Publishing under the author name S. Carlisle May. She has written over thirty books in her career.

Contact with the Author

I hope you enjoyed my story. If you did, I would appreciate you leaving a review on Amazon, Barnes and Noble, or Goodreads.

You can stay in touch with me at any of the addresses below. I love to hear from my readers.

http://www.SusanCarlisle.com – Join my newsletter here

http://www.Facebook.com/SusanCarlisle

http://www.Twitter.com/SusanCarlisle1

http://www.Instrgram.com/SusanCarlisle

http://www.SusanCMay.com

http://www.WWIIArmyAirForceMedicine.com

Made in the USA
Coppell, TX
13 October 2023

22774150R00131